God's Not Finished With Me Yet

Also by Brian C. Johnson, PhD

Finding God in the Bathroom

God's Not Finished With Me Yet

a novel

Rev. Brian C. Johnson, PhD

WordCrafts Press

Love Lifted Me
James Rowe, 1912
Public Domain

Nothing but the Blood of Jesus
Robert Lowry, 1876
Public Domain

God's Not Finished With Me Yet is a work of fiction. The author has endeavored to be respectful to all persons, places, and events presented in this novel. Still, this is a novel, and all references to persons, places and events are fictitious or used fictitiously.

*I'm so grateful to my wife, Darlene, and my children.
Thank you for believing in me and encouraging me
to carry this writing mantle.*

Why is it so freaking difficult to exit away from a porn site? I can't be the only one sneaking a peek, so I can imagine the sites' creators could devise a quicker, easier escape hatch. All these stupid pop-ups—are they really necessary?

Amid the panic of being caught—literally—with my pants down, I managed to close the last pop-up box as Camille rounded the corner of the den. She saw my laptop open on my lap and asked me what I was doing.

"I'm just checking my email. What's up?"

"And what have you been doing all day?" she queried.

"I had a meeting earlier with Pastor; after that, not much, just chilling. What's for dinner?"

"Why are you asking me? You've been home all day and didn't cook? Why do I have to be the only one who cooks in this house? You know how to cook!"

"I don't know what you want. You didn't leave me a note like you usually do."

"You are so helpless. Oh my God, why can't you make a decision on your own? Just cook something for goodness sakes! I'm not that hard to please."

In my mind, I retorted, *Oh please, yes you are!* But I dared not speak those words aloud. As she slammed cabinet and pantry doors, I could hear slight mumbles of titles I'd heard before, "Useless! Worthless!" With each slam, the daggers pierced deeper. I felt small like the tiniest doll in the Matryoshka. Each ingredient she frustratingly poured or sprinkled made me worry about my safety.

Later, after the dinner dishes were washed, dried, and put away, and the kids were tucked into bed, I stole away to the den for some quiet time of my own. It was my turn to preach, and I should have been preparing a long time ago. I reasoned it best to stay out of her way. Didn't take long until I was filling out my own profile on a dating site for lonely singles. Those infomercials made it seem like there were hundreds of lonely people looking for a romantic interlude, or just wanting to *get down and dirty* without a lot of strings. At that moment, I didn't think it would lead to anything real. It was just intriguing. I was also kinda curious—nosy, if the truth be told—and wanted to see if there were any faces I recognized among the pictures.

There were.

There were several people I immediately recognized—one was a former student. His profile suggested MSM (man seeking man). The revelation floored me. I didn't know the guy was gay, but I couldn't share my find with my wife. I'm pretty sure she would question what I was doing prowling around that dating site to begin with. Not really a discussion I was prepared to have right then.

When Camille and I argued, I found it easy to retreat into virtual relationships. I blamed her. It was her fault. *She drove me to this,* I reasoned inside my head. It was much easier to place the blame on someone else rather than search deeper within myself for an answer. I didn't want to confront the vast emptiness inside. I felt the need to fill that void, but with what was something that escaped me. And I wasn't sure I wanted to know the answer.

I kept looking over my shoulder at every sound. I hated how jumpy I had become. But my anxiety would melt away as I became engrossed in the bouncing and thrusting appearing on my computer monitor. I was the biggest sucker for how the videos were titled. I wondered about whose job it was to watch and categorize each video and come up with unique ways of tagging them: *Ebony, Babe, Teen, Threesome, Japanese, Babysitter, Interracial*—just about any and every nationality, hair color, body type, or fetish. There seemed to be no end to what was available. Some sites only held my interest for brief periods; others held me captive. I was particularly wary of the ones requiring emails or credit card numbers in order to view anything. I worried about leaving a bread crumb trail that could lead back to me somehow. The sites offering free looks got my attention. The first sites were nothing but still pictures, but as technology advanced, still pics gave way to short videos.

She doesn't deserve the blame, but my first visit to an *adult* store was with my beautiful bride. She always was the adventurous type, and she was interested in adding some spice to our boudoir activities. She—well, *we*—wanted to get a toy to tickle her a little better than I was able. It was obvious that we were neophytes the way we kept watching the clerk and jumping when the door opened. But I was astounded at the hundreds of DVDs and magazines. Racks of nakedness confronted our eyes, but it was the titles that intrigued me.

"Babe, look at this one. It's called *Tiger's Wood*." The black man standing near a scantily clad white girl was meant to evoke images of Tiger and his European wife, Elin.

She picked up a copy of *Buttman and Robin* and chuckled over the bad costuming. "I wonder if they have to pay the movie companies. These are obviously plays on the real movies."

"Where do they get this stuff?" I had already picked up a new DVD with the title of *Breast Side Story*. There was one that depicted an African American soldier in military uniform with his junk exposed, and the title was a play on words with male genitalia and the film *Blackhawk Down*. I could not ignore the one that read *Saving Ryan's Privates* with the crouched naked soldier trying to shield himself with his hands. His pectoral muscles had been oiled and were glistening in the sunlight.

By the time we found the toy section, we were drunk with giddiness at the campiness of all that we had considered. I stored some of the titles in my mental Rolodex—*for later*. Over the years, we have stopped at other adult shops together, but we never had the guts to venture behind the special curtain where we saw individual guys sneak through.

"I wonder what goes on back there?" Camille queried.

I answered, "I have no idea, but I'm sure it's not good.

We walked away with our prize—a vibrating blue dolphin in a box titled, LOVE. I should have taken it as an omen that the thing started smoking and sparking during our first use.

2

Sunday morning we went to church as usual. The worship team had just finished singing, and the offering had been collected. Pastor Craft ascended the pulpit.

"On this Sunday, we are in for a rare treat. Our own youth pastor is going to be blessing us with the word. Pastor Bobby J, come on up here and give us what thus saith the Lord."

"Have you ever wrestled with God? I have." I greeted the parishioners as I took my place behind the pulpit.

You see, my sermon was about the importance of being honest with yourself and sharing your struggles with others. I was planning to invite those who were proud of their deliverance to join me on the platform, but how could I reciprocate given my hidden proclivities? I felt an urging in my spirit to admit my struggle. I thought, *Surely you can't mean me? I can't tell them.*

All night long, I had tossed and turned as I wrestled with my decision. To say "Yes" was to admit weakness and defeat, but I couldn't really imagine telling God "No." Regardless, I did as I was asked. I stood and admitted I was weak—repeatedly. In my experience, Christians do not take admitting fault too kindly. What would they think of me—one of their pastors?

I had stood up from my seat in the second pew, my feet feeling like lead. I had never any problem preaching before. These people loved me. They seemed to really enjoy the simplicity of my messages. I'm pretty sure they weren't ready for what I was going to lay on them this morning.

I opened my mouth to speak, but nothing came out. I let out a huge sigh. "Whew, I'm nervous. My hands are so sweaty."

A chorus of "Let Him use you" and "That's alright, baby" rang out in encouragement from some of the elder women.

I paused in wonder. *How do I tell them? What will they say? How will they react?* Those were just some of the thoughts racing through my head as I stood before my congregation preparing to tell them my deepest, darkest secret.

As is customary, I prayed before beginning. "God, I am your vessel. The words I say today, I believe are what you have for your people. Take me and hide me behind the cross. Let them see you and not me. And now, Dear Father, let the words of my mouth and the meditation of my heart be acceptable in thy sight, O Lord, my strength and my Redeemer. In Jesus' name. And all of God's people said, Amen."

Amens rang out all over the church.

Ever since the Old Testament, the children of Israel had been following an honesty policy. This policy included public repentance. In Judaism, there are three steps in repentance. The first is to regret the wrongdoing. The second is to orally confess the sin, and the third expected one to turn from wickedness. I had done steps one and three multiple times, but number two was a doozy!

Wouldn't God accept that I had gone part-way by doing two of the required steps? Could I really be healed by doing things my own way? Then I read Psalm 32:1–5

> *Blessed is he whose transgression is forgiven, whose sin is covered.*
> *Blessed is the man unto whom the Lord imputeth not iniquity, and in whose spirit there is no guile.*
> *When I kept silence, my bones waxed old through my roaring all the day long.*
> *For day and night thy hand was heavy upon me: my moisture is turned into the drought of summer. Selah.*
> *I acknowledge my sin unto thee, and mine iniquity have I not hid. I said, I will confess my transgressions unto the Lord; and thou forgavest the iniquity of my sin.*

But God knows my thoughts, right? Why do I need to make it public? These verses in Psalms dictated the need to tell—to make it plain—to speak aloud and let go of the poison. No more covering, no more hiding. I would do it God's way.

Breathy and my voice shaking, I jumped in. I had never been so nervous. I felt like I was swallowing my stomach. I had worn my serious black suit and tie. Normally I wear flannel shirts and jeans. The kids don't care what I wear—anything except a suit. But today I wanted to be taken seriously.

As a youth minister, I typically use personal stories, object lessons, and interactive exercises to emphasize my messages. To illustrate my point, I called for volunteers of those who had testimonies of deliverance from past addictions to join me down front. "Is there anybody here who has ever done anything they regret?" Hands were raised all over the congregation. "Is there anybody here who has failed God at some point?" More hands. "Perhaps you are here today, and you don't mind publicly admitting you've made some mistakes, maybe even some *on-purposes*. Don't worry, I'm not going to ask you to testify about your failures. You don't have to put your business in the street. What I am looking for today are people who will admit they've done wrong, and God has delivered them. If that's you, come on down here and join me around this platform."

At least twenty-five people had flanked the stage around me. I sighed and invited the congregation to turn in their Bibles to my scripture text for that morning Hebrews 11:2.

"When you have it, say, *Amen*. I waited a few seconds until the amens started to die down. I read it slowly to the congregation.

Wherefore seeing we also are compassed about with so great a cloud of witnesses, let us lay aside every weight, and the sin which doth so easily beset us, and let us run with patience the race that is set before us.

The whole point of the message was the importance of learning from the mistakes of others and that discipleship included accountability in relationships. There I was, surrounded by people who were unashamed to say that they were a part of the cloud; and yet, there I was, quivering.

Standing there on that four-by-four platform behind the ivory pulpit that looked like it had been passed down from Westminster Abbey, my mind flashed back to the numerous times I had watched that Jimmy Swaggart confessional video on the internet.

There he stood in his serious black suit and tie—much like I was dressed that day—and confessed his affair with the prostitute. Tears running down his face and his Southern drawl on display, "I have sinned against you, my Lord." To be honest, I had laughed as I watched him beg for the forgiveness of his wife, Francis; how he wept bitter tears as he sobbed, the television camera panned to the on-looking parishioners who wiped sad tears with white tissues. An elder sitting in the pulpit was visibly shaking trying to hold back his tears. A robed choir member held his head in his hands as he tried to compose himself. There Swaggart stood, a giant of the faith—caught in his sin. Jim Carrey masterfully mimicked this whole testimony as he portrayed Reverend Carl Pathos on *In Living Color*.

Equally funny to me, for some reason, was the footage of Jim Bakker being dragged from his home by federal marshals after his arrest for defrauding his *PTL* investors. His affair with Jessica Hahn had been made public. I swore I would *never* be like those poor slobs.

Caught!

They were found out.

I would not be like that.

For years, I had successfully hid my voyeuristic proclivities, but here I was...telling on myself. Not because I was fighting off some media firestorm, but because "God told me to." My own free will— of my own volition.

My point had already been made; I had 25 powerful examples— testimonies of deliverance from alcohol, crack cocaine, heroin, and prescription drug addictions. This congregation did not need to hear that one of their ministers had suffered—was still suffering—from a serious pornography addiction. They didn't need to know that at times I would leave the pulpit and spend hours surfing the dark side of the internet. They had already had enough of the national scandals featuring prominent ministers who had very public falls from grace; they certainly did not need an example this close to home.

This will just kill them. I imagined the faces of those young adults and teenagers whom I had been mentoring. *How can I hurt them by exposing my shame? If they only knew what I was really like, what I struggle with every day, the kinds of thoughts I entertained this week.*

I preached, "We all have a past. We all come from somewhere. Moses had a past—none of us was born perfect. Oh, I know your mothers thought you were just the cutest, most precious, most adorable, perfect little being ever."

People started pointing at each other and snickering. *I'm making connections.*

"But we all have a past." *The snickering ceased.*

"If you think about it, Moses' story is a colorful one. Born under a death sentence, he was abandoned by his mother, who packed him up in a basket and sent him down the river. In what could be called a stroke of good fortune, a princess of Egypt just happened to be bathing in the river and pulled him out. Raised to be in the lineage of the Pharaoh, it was all taken away in an instant. You know the story—Moses saw one of the Hebrew slaves being mistreated by an overseer and killed the taskmaster. An abandoned baby turned prince of Egypt who became a murderer."

Deacon Pettigrew chimed in, "You talking right, brother." He pointed his finger in my direction as he spoke.

"Moses ran away in shame; I am not sure why. As prince, he probably could have exonerated himself or at least justified the killing; but he tucked his tail and ran to the backside of a mountain. There he tended sheep for forty years." I paused for effect before starting anew. "The life of a shepherd is a lonely one with plenty of time to rehearse the mistakes of his past. I can imagine moments of paranoia as he speculated that soldiers would appear at any moment to come drag him back to face his crimes. I can just see him nervously looking over his shoulder the first couple of years."

I certainly know what that's like. Having a secret habit teaches you a thing or two about the fear of getting caught.

I paused for emphasis. "Perhaps on a cold night, Moses had a moment to reflect upon his past. Perhaps he wondered how he got there. 'I was a prince; an heir to the throne of Egypt—what am I doing out here sleeping next to a pile of sheep dung?' Imagine—an abandoned baby poised to become a future king who became a

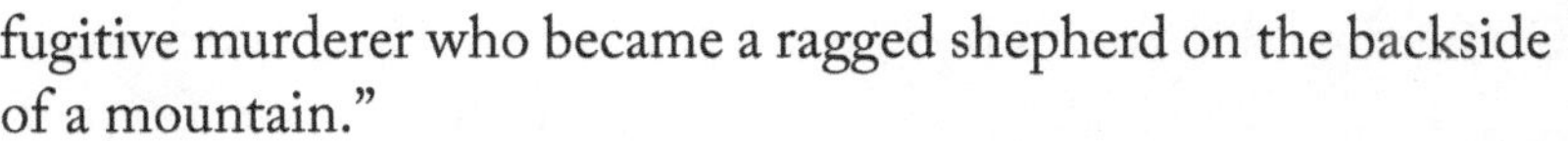

fugitive murderer who became a ragged shepherd on the backside of a mountain."

Oh, how many times I sat at that computer and felt like a total failure—I had made that promise that I would never *do it again—if He would just forgive me just this one last time.*

I had reasoned… *Mine is the tale of loneliness and shame--of suffering in silence. I felt like I couldn't tell anyone what I was going through. It was a selfish fear, I know, but the mere thought of someone knowing my crushing failure was paralyzing.*

But, there I was at my burning bush—standing there in front of the congregation. I exhorted them, "James 5:16 says, 'Confess your faults one to another, and pray for one another, that ye may be healed.' Each one of those folks standing near me on this platform have "overcome by the blood of the lamb and the word of their testimony."

And here I stand listening at the voice of the Lord telling me, like Moses, to essentially go back to the place of my greatest failure.

I continued. "The Almighty spoke to Moses about His concern for the children of Israel because of their bonds. It was strange enough to be talking to a bush that actually talked back."

There were a few chuckles throughout the crowd.

"But in that moment when God was saying that He is ready to make His big move—I can imagine that Moses' life flashed before his eyes. He responded just like I would have. Moses basically said, "You want me to do *what?* Me? You know my story; abandoned baby, prince of a foreign nation, cold-blooded killer on the lam, old shepherd hiding out on a hill in the middle of a desert. Are you sure you want *me?*"

OK, Bobby. Point of no return. Put up or shut up time.

"Like so many, I have struggles. Your struggle may be different than mine. But, I'm sick of hiding."

I named it—Pornography.

Standing there, I explained to two hundred people that for nearly twenty-five years I had been hiding my problem.

I tried not to make eye contact with anyone because I anticipated the looks of disappointment. I did give a passing glance in Pastor

Craft's direction and fully expected that he would not-so-politely pull me off the platform and scourge me right there in front of everyone. Those elderly grandmas who were always telling me how much they loved me—I just knew they were clutching their pearls in shocked disgust.

I finished the sermon in tears. "There's not much more I can say other than, pray for me, because I need it." I took my seat with my head down. Pastor Craft walked slowly to assume my position behind the rostrum, and I prepared for the worst. Instead, he thanked me for my honesty and stepped down from the platform. As he approached me, I felt dread and panic. Yet, instead of the public flogging I felt I deserved, he stood directly in front of me.

He said, "Stand up, Pastor Bobby J." And he wrapped his arms around me. He encouraged the congregation to hear the message of accountability as an essential tool in our journey towards spiritual victory.

When church was over, no one treated me unkindly; the grandmas still loved on me. At least fifty people hugged me afterwards and thanked me for sharing my story, some of them admitting similar struggles. I looked to the right and saw Sister Lucy eight months pregnant and waddling in my direction. She hugged me tightly. "Pastor Bobby, that sermon was amazing! I've never seen a preacher admit even getting a hangnail—let alone dealing with real problems like that." Her breath was hot in my ear. She pulled back and kept talking, but quietly like she was sharing a secret. "Can I tell you something? Brett, my husband, I think deals with the same problem you do. He doesn't know that I know, but would you please keep him in your prayers?" We talked for a while, but before she left, she made sure to tell me, "Please don't tell him I told you."

Later in his encounter with Moses, God asked Moses an important question— "What is that in your hand?" It was the tool of a shepherd—the shepherd who bore the stain of past failures—it was that very tool God would use to show His great power and deliver a people. So, there he was—abandoned baby, turned prince, turned fugitive murderer, turned shepherd on the backside of a mountain—who became the savior of a people because he dared to have his past transformed by an amazing God. That sermon was my attempt at following in Moses' footsteps. My rod is my story of freedom; I hoped my sharing the struggle could be used to free the parishioners and their loved ones.

As we prepared to depart, Pastor Craft came up to me and whispered, "Pastor Bobby, can I see you in my office for a few minutes?" I sheepishly agreed.

My inner monologue played in my head.

I knew it. He was just being too nice back there. He didn't want to embarrass me in front of the congregation. He was saving his tirade for a private meeting.

I entered his quarters like a middle schooler being called into the vice principal's office—humility and fear weighing me down. I quickly took a seat in one of the faux leather desk chairs—one of four surrounding his desk. He entered the office, closing the door behind him, and I patiently waited in fearful expectation. He didn't say much as he removed his black cleric's robes; for a moment, I was eight years old again waiting for the lash of the belt.

"Bobby J." My government name was Reverend Robert John Tompkins.

Like a little child I moaned out, "I'm so sorry, Pastor. I'm ashamed of myself. I understand if you want to set me down."

"I meant what I said out there." A semi-smile creaked at the corner of his mouth. "What you did today took courage, humility, and a great deal of integrity."

Integrity was a descriptor I would never have used for myself, particularly with the memories of my illicit viewing the evening before playing in my head.

"Don't get me wrong. I can't excuse your moral failure, but honesty like you just revealed is unheard of in the church today, and I applaud what you've done. Undoubtedly, my phone will be ringing off the hook this week. There will be those who'll want your head on a post, but all I want from you is a hug."

"A hug? Don't you want to yell at me? I just belied your faith and trust in front of the whole church." The large photo of his family—his wife and children—those same children in the youth group I led weekly, bore holes in my spectacled face. I readjusted my tie that suddenly felt like a boa constrictor tightening its coils.

He leaned forward in his chair. "Trying to hide a moral failure or failing to disclose the entire truth sometimes leads to rumors that are far more damaging than the truth," he warned. "You can't sweep it under the rug," he stressed. "A lot of preachers think they're protecting the congregation by hiding the truth, but in so doing they're actually denying what Jesus said. It's the truth that'll set people free. Let me ask you like Jesus asked the man at Bethesda, Do you want to get well?"

"I do, Pastor; I'm sick of living like this." My voice broke as I begged.

"Then give me access to your life. You need to continually be honest with me and call me when you're struggling—you have my number—I don't care what time of day or night, we'll pray and ask the Lord to give you the strength to stand. When I ask you how you are doing, I'm not really asking about the weather. I want to know *how* you are holding up. I want real accountability. If you're feeling weak, admit it. If you fail, accept the responsibility. We'll get you back on track."

He paused. "How is your wife handling all this?"

Coils.

3

Standing up to leave, I said, "Thank you, Pastor. I appreciate your support. It means a lot." I stood up feeling oddly refreshed.

"Hang in there. We love you. I'll be praying for you."

I left Pastor Craft's office feeling pretty good about myself. It had been ages since I had felt good about anything really. I wanted to feel pride, but it's hard to feel proud of yourself by reveling in your own moral failure. I was glad to have a true spiritual father who was going to help me get better—one who had not condemned me to burn in hell's fires. Honestly, I was doing that just fine on my own.

I turned left to go downstairs to meet my wife, Camille, but as I descended, she was coming up the stairs. Her eyes pierced my soul.

"What in the world did you preach about?"

Camille had duty in the children's church that day. Normally, she was at all my sermons. She sat on the second pew, my forever *Amen Corner*. But today, it was just me and the onlookers. "I've had a bunch of people stop me and tell me they were praying for me. A couple of them even interrupted my class. 'Sister Camille, I'm sorry to cut in, but I want you to know that I'm here for you if you need to talk.' Sister Evelyn just came in to give me a hug.' What in the world is going on?"

Trying to be flippant and change the subject, I said, "Where do you want to eat today? I'm sure hungry."

"Seriously, quit playing. What did you talk about?" Camille was not one for surprises.

I was OK with my revelation upstairs with the pastor, but now I was faced with telling the one person who would be the most heartbroken, who would be the most ashamed of me. "I told them that I struggled with a porn addiction."

"You did *what*?!"

In those brief moments, I rethought my entire message. Did I do and say the right thing?

"What do you mean, porn addiction? When? Where? I didn't know you looked at that stuff!"

Wanting to be honest, I continued, "I'm sorry, babe. It's pretty bad."

"And you told the congregation—*before* you told me?"

"I was just so ashamed. I couldn't tell you."

If looks could kill.

"You couldn't tell me, but you could tell hundreds of people *in church*?" She began to cry, and my heart positively broke. "I can't believe you would do that to me! How could you betray me like this?"

"I was preaching about accountability, and I just felt like God wanted me to be honest with the people. I didn't *want* to say anything, but the Spirit wouldn't let me go."

"Don't go blaming God! You did this. You! Not God." She moaned a little bit as she wiped away the tears and began stomping up the stairs.

I now wished I had communicated with her and shared not only what I was going to be preaching about, but what I had been dealing with for so long. She was my best friend, my closest confidante and I had failed her—*big time*. And now, she would be faced with the task of cleaning up behind my elephant. I tried to be OK with rationalizing *for better or worse* from our marriage vows, but honestly, in this moment, I knew I had already broken those vows.

The walk to the parking lot was slow. My feet just didn't want to go. I buckled the kids into their car seats in silence. We usually go out to eat on Sundays after church, but I just drove past our regular haunt. We drove home in silence. The children tried to engage us in conversation, but we hushed them into discomfort. Pain filled my face as I glanced uneasily at the hurt and disgust Camille wore on her face. I had really messed up this time.

Our home was only three miles from the church, but that minivan ride seemed to take forever. I didn't want it to end, however;

the thought of being alone with Camille in this condition was not attractive to me at all. When we started into our driveway, I imagined our blue front door as the sliding cell doors in a prison. I could sense that I was walking into my own personal hell—one of my own creation—I had awakened a very real monster, and I was going to have to face it head on.

I took out my keys and opened the door. I pushed the dog back inside. She always tries to escape when the door opens. As is my habit when she is angry, I hid from Camille for a while feigning busyness. For all her sweetness, she can be a really scary lady. She is all business when she wants to be, and I had unleashed the beast.

I went to the pantry and started to make PB&J and Cheetos for the kids. It wasn't a traditional Sunday meal, but they had to eat. I wasn't all that hungry, so I disappeared from the kitchen as soon as I could.

This self-imposed stalemate needs to come to an end.

I was sitting in the easy chair—*hah, easy!*—in the living room when she sat down nearby.

"Why don't you love me?"

"That's a stupid question," I responded idiotically. "I do love you."

"Then, why I am not enough for you?"

"Oh, c'mon, baby," I sweetly intoned. "You're more than enough for me."

"Then why are you looking at those women? Are you not attracted to me anymore?"

I leaned in to kiss her tear-streaked face despite her attempts to pull away, "Babe, you are my sole reason for living."

She backed up curtly. Arguing, "I can't be if you are spending God only knows how many hours looking at that filth!"

"Listen, I don't know why I do it, but I know it has absolutely nothing to do with you."

I spaced out for a moment as I thought about my life.

My relationship with pornography began when I was just a kid, maybe eight years old. My brothers and I shared a paper route. My elder brother had mentioned that inside the mail slot of the machine shop near our childhood playground there were pictures of naked ladies on the wall. I had not yet found my true interest in girls or women, but the thought of seeing naked images was titillating, even to my young mind. I remember the feeling between my legs when I watched Angie Dickinson in *Big, Bad Mama* about the pistol-packing lady and her daughters. That movie was my first exposure to female nudity. Mama was hell-bent on protecting her daughters' innocence and did not want them to be corrupted by the world. Little did she know—*or maybe she did*—that those few scenes would be the start of my affliction that would not be healed for decades.

Back then, movies like that one did not come on regular TV. Long before pay-per-view and DVD, premium movies were only possible through a three-button decoder box that descrambled the pay channels. Pubescent boys, like and me and my brothers would remember trying to catch a glimpse of naked female parts through the scrambled channels. My history of stolen glances at naked women could probably be traced to those misadventures when late at night, my brothers and I would sneak downstairs to the family TV room to cover the buttons with a pillow to drown out the sound of the loud click that boomed when one of the buttons was pressed. Some nights, momma heard the click and yelled for us to go to bed. Stealing away got much easier with the advent of the internet.

In those days, we settled for the magazine cutouts like at the machine shop. It was near the end of the route and seeing the prize took skill as one needed to get low in front of the door and pry open the mail slot without making too much noise as to alert the workers inside. If you were careful enough, a few ladies were displayed across the walls.

At other times, spending the nights with neighborhood friends would almost guarantee that one of the older boys would pull out a magazine pilfered from one of their father's collections. If not, they at least knew about a hidden spot where a *Playboy* or *Penthouse* was skillfully stashed. Oddly, no one ever seemed to mind sharing the details of availability. That openness of exchange would change later, when viewing porn became more of a private, solo act rather than a communal joint activity.

For several years after that, I can't seem to recall a habit of looking at forbidden porn. Sure, I got off by watching softcore R-rated movies, but those were harmless, right? A few eager glances at risqué material would not amount to anything, would they? I was certainly spiritually strong enough to handle a few breasts, right?

I was first introduced to masturbation by watching porn. I had never done it myself—the act was forbidden by the church. It was the *sin of Onan* for goodness sakes. In this one movie, there was a guy who was pretending to be a butler, and he had made a salad for his mistress. She was in her bedroom working her magic on another dude. Perhaps the butler guy got mad, but soon, he had added his own special dressing to the salad mix. I admit it, I was intrigued by the act. To that point, my only experiences with ejaculation were nocturnal and beyond my control. Taking matters in my own hands, so to speak, began an all-new life practice for me.

Soon, it was an overwhelming thirst. It was uncontrollable. I just *had* to do it. I started searching for weird places to be alone to practice my art. Once, when I was sixteen, I was riding the city bus to work at a local fast food place. When the other riders got off, so did I. I can remember the scene in *Basketball Diaries* when Jim (Leonardo DiCaprio) and his sick friend discussed the numerous times they whacked. It turned into a contest. That same day, I found myself with a few free moments near the supply sink in the back of the restaurant.

I thought the true depth of my depravity was revealed when I did it at church. My youth group was at the church having rehearsal for our annual Christmas pageant. I excused myself to the restroom and managed to squeeze one out in time to return to rehearsal. I had hit rock bottom—or so I thought. All the usual pleasure was gone; it was just an action. No joy, no fun, just an act of will; I prayed that night for forgiveness—and help. I clearly needed help. The pastors and visiting evangelists often referred to having a reprobate mind. I was convinced that I had crossed some spiritual line towards degeneracy. I tried to stop. I really wanted to stop. No force of willpower seemed to help. I was a pervert. I needed something stronger.

I didn't stop feeding the beast, however. I recall a scripture passage in the Gospels where Jesus talked about a strong man coming back into a clean temple with seven worse spirits. *Was I possessed?* That was a question I asked, but really didn't want to know the answer to.

According to teen boy culture, I started dating late. I was fourteen by the time I got a real girlfriend. The young lady I chose was much more experienced than I. In fact, she had been one of my brother's former concubines. I was awed by him; he was older than me, and he would attract his fair share of ladies. Honestly, he treated them poorly, so I, the mayor of the Friend Zone, would nurse them back to health.

Angela had been with my brother, but she was an acceptable candidate. Heck, she accepted me; that was really the only criterion. I desperately wanted somebody—anybody—to love me. My brother's leftovers were a delicacy in my skewed psyche. In my mixed-up head, I loved her. I realize now that my need to emulate my brother's folly had fooled me into thinking I could do more, get away with more. I had seen and wanted what he was doing on the church bus with his girlfriends, wanted what he had been doing with them in the hotel rooms of church conventions. I didn't want to be the lookout anymore. I just didn't want to be the goody two-shoed church boy anymore. I would have my turn.

Angela and I had a couple brief encounters, but nothing significant, or so I convinced myself. We kissed deeply and passionately—a lot. She let me touch her under parts on a couple occasions. One day I went over her house when her mom wasn't home. She answered the door in her nightgown, and I could see her lady parts were unshackled. I pounced. We soon were interrupted by the sound of her mother's car in the driveway.

Angela jumped up. "My mom's home. You better hide. Quick!" She pulled me by the arm and stashed me in the garage where her family's Doberman viciously barked and strained against his chains in my direction. I could hear her mother fussing and wondering why she was still in her nightgown and not fully dressed. Soon, Angela came out and rescued me and pushed me out the garage's side door. She slipped me a little tongue as she pushed.

"I love you. I promise I'll make it up to you."

Perhaps I should have taken that as a sign from God, but sadly, I ignored the hint. I still had not had my turn.

My turn came one cold winter. To earn free lunch and ice cream in school, I sold milk for the cafeteria ladies. I sat at a table outside the cafeteria a few minutes before the lunch period. There was a young lady who bought milk from me every day. I didn't really talk to her or know her at all. One particular day in February, she cast me that *come hither* smile when she bought her milk. I wondered about her. When she came to my table the next day, I struck up a conversation with her. Her name was Spring. The very next day, we had sex in the storage locker of the school gymnasium. No real relationship and no questions asked.

I walked home in shame. That evening, we were having revival services at the church. I sat quietly through the evening's services, despite our fiery Pentecostal experience. I couldn't shake the feeling of condemnation—that feeling that told me I was going straight to hell. The speaker's message included the verse from Romans 8 about *no condemnation in Christ*. It would not be the last time I used the scriptures to rationalize my sin.

Camille interrupted my thought process. "So, why am I not enough for you?"

4

"Bobby J, I'd like to meet with you in my office tomorrow at 2:00." The caller ID and familiar voice of my pastor beckoned on the phone.

"Sure, I can be there," I simply responded. Tomorrow was Thursday. I was off on Thursdays.

His motorcycle was in his parking space when I arrived. Yes, he is that cool. I knocked on the door and walked in. I took the first chair and sat down quickly. The smiling eyes from the family picture were still there.

"Bobby J, how are things at home?"

"To be honest, Pastor," I sighed, "Not good. Camille blames herself for my problem. I tried to convince her that it's my own sickness, my own shame, but she remains unmoved."

Pastor Craft inquired, "How would you describe your relationship with the Lord?"

"Wow, that shouldn't be a tough question. I've been saved since I was a young kid, but frankly, I'm not really sure. I feel I've gone too far." The shame flooded my heart.

"I want to assure you of something. Nothing we can do is greater than what God has planned for us! It's exciting. You should anticipate His blessings. Wait for Him! King Solomon in Ecclesiastes 1:14 said, *Nothing can satisfy the entire man but the Lord's love and the Lord Himself.* In his own words, he said, *I tried everything, searched everywhere and found nothing but weariness of spirit.*"

Pastor Craft continued, "Charles Spurgeon preached, *...if you roam the world around, you will see no sights like...the Savior's face; if you could have all the comforts of life, but lost your Savior, you would be wretched; but if you win Christ, then should you rot in a dungeon, you* *would find it a paradise; should you live in obscurity, or die with famine, you will yet be satisfied with favor and be full of the goodness of God."*

"That all sounds well and good, Pastor, but how do I stop? I have been battling this for many years now, and frankly, I'm tired of losing."

I should have expected his next question.

"How often do you study the Word?"

Ouch! For a minister, my answer should have been, *Daily—every day, I study the Bible.* Truthfully, I had to admit, "Not nearly as much as I should. Mostly, right before I have to preach."

"There's part of your problem right there. Psalm 119:9 says, *Wherewithal shall a young man cleanse his way? By taking heed thereto according to thy word."*

I swear the man was a walking Bible.

"Do you hear that? You won't be able to stop until you find yourself immersed in God's Word."

I sarcastically responded. "The Bible can't stop me from looking at porn. I'm broken. I'm damaged goods."

Ever ready with an answer, Pastor declared, "David was also a broken man with faults. He lusted after Bathsheba and had her husband killed so that he could have her. Yet, the Scriptures call him *a man after God's own heart.* What about the Apostle Paul? He wrote two-thirds of the New Testament and yet in the book of Romans describes his own personal war within himself. He calls himself wretched and cries out for deliverance. And you can't tell me all that wanton sexuality in Greece didn't impact him. I mean, they worshipped Aphrodite, the goddess of sex."

He was right. I had preached that same message before. I let my mind drift. I recalled a message I once delivered titled "The Swimming Lesson." The thoughts flashed through my mind of my preaching. I had likened our spiritual walk to playing in a swimming pool. My text had come from the book of Ezekiel 47.

✝✝✝

"Remember the plastic pool we all had when we were kids? An ankle deep spiritual relationship can be likened to the baby pool.

And what do we remember about being in the baby pool—playing and splashing around. Spiritually, being in ankle deep water is a relationship with God that is about conviction. When we are convicted, we are in a place of guilt and judgment. When we are at this level, it is easy to come to church. In this state, when I feel like attending the service, or if I just come to hear the singing, or when there's an altar call, I only get close enough to splash around. Or maybe I am satisfied to get a touch from the Lord. That ankle-deep relationship is all about fun—it's not about changing. You expect the Lord to bless you, but you don't expect to have to change your behavior or give up anything in return. Some of us are right there—playing with the Lord."

Amens rang out all over the church.

"The angel says that this is not enough and directs us to a deeper level. He measures out an additional line to where the water comes to the knees. It is important to note that the water is at the knees because typically this is the place of humility in prayer—we kneel before God in the submissive act of repentance. A part of the process of repentance is acknowledging that I am in a sinful state, and I am standing in the face of an holy God. In a sinful state, we are unable to continue in the presence of the Lord (Psalm 24), so we have to humble ourselves to be exalted through repentance.

This stage is still pretty shallow. The water is just to the knees—which leaves plenty of room to splash and play. Now, don't get me wrong, repenting from our sins is important, but we must be willing to go beyond repentance. In fact, the scriptures teach us in Hebrews 6:

Therefore leaving the principles of the doctrine of Christ, let us go on unto perfection; not laying again the foundation of repentance from dead works, and of faith toward God, Of the doctrine of baptisms, and of laying on of hands, and of resurrection of the dead, and of eternal judgment.

The angel of the Lord leads us to a deeper place than repentance. The man measures out another 1000 cubits—1750 feet—and the waters come to the level of our loins. Now we're starting to get somewhere. Now, we're getting ready to go in the deep end of the pool. We're crossing the line demarcating the swimmers from the novices. At this stage the water is about waist high. The spiritual description for this stage is conversion.

In the book of Acts, Peter gives the instructions—*Repent and be converted that your sins may be blotted out*. What does it mean to be converted? The loins. This region is the area where our nature resides. It is the place from which life flows—think biologically."

I drew an imaginary circle around my nether region.

"Women birth children from the loins—men plant seeds of life from their loins. Our nature can be described as our primitive state, our fundamental disposition or temperament. Our human nature and predisposition is such that it is typically opposite from God's. Paul mentioned that our flesh often wars with the spirit—a constant struggle of good versus evil. To convert means to change—and this is what God wants. The water at the loins means we are being converted and changed from what we used to be. When we are—born again the scriptures teach us that we—put on Christ and are made anew. Further, when Christ returns, we'll be changed again—we'll shed this mortal and put on immortality—corruptible will put on incorruptible. It is good thing to submit to the will of God and allow God to change us, but still that's not enough. Somebody say, 'It's not enough!'"

Voices rang out in the call and response.

"Now… Having your nature changed is a constant struggle, so the spirit leads us to a deeper place where we are no longer in control. The waters are deep enough to swim in. In the deepest waters, the current is so strong that even the strongest swimmers have difficulty going against where the water leads. Spiritually, this is the place of sanctification. Now we're swimming. God would have our relationships with him at this level. At this stage, we are no longer reliant on our own powers and abilities. In Romans 12, verse 2, Paul refers to this process as being—*transformed by the renewing of your mind*. This mind renewal is so that we can be assured of knowing that which is good, acceptable, and perfect, and in the will of the Lord for your life. Secret sin is none of these things.

"Now… It's in this place where my mind is renewed, where I am no longer in control and am being led by the Spirit, that I am stronger than my weaknesses. The Apostle Paul stated that—*in my flesh, there is no good thing.* So, by myself, I cannot control me. Willpower alone is insufficient. Although you must make the choice to live righteously; your will must be subject to God's will. Solomon stated, in Proverbs 3:5, that we are not to—*lean on our own understanding,* because we are faulty. This notion of sanctification requires us to yield to God's authority and direction. In water rescue training, lifeguards are taught to teach the struggling or drowning person to surrender to the current and allow it to carry them; fighting against the current only makes you tired.

"In the deeper waters, the heart is covered. The heart is the seat of our wills and emotions. It is also the place where all blood flows—the sustainer of life. If the heart stops, life ceases to be. This reflects a necessity of having a heart change. Interestingly enough, several times in the Greek translations of scripture, the word *mind* is the same as the word *heart.* So, having a renewed and transformed mind may also be referring to having a pure heart."

✝✝✝

Pastor Craft continued. *Had he been talking this whole time?* "In Psalm 51, David prayed, *Create in me a clean heart, O God, and renew a right spirit within me.* This is why it is easy for people to go back into sin—their heart has not been renewed, and the right spirit is not present. If the heart is impure, then everything that ensues from it is also impure."

"Yup, that's me. A man with an impure heart." My remorse was getting the better of me.

"And aren't you glad we serve *the* heart-fixer?"

We talked for a while. It seemed like he was just checking in. Nothing major. I said goodbye to the pastor and returned home. When I got to the house, I sat down at the desk and turned on the computer to check my email. I was feeling empowered by my meeting, operative word *was.* Of all the titles in the subject lines of my email account, I zeroed in on the one titled *Nude Pics Of Angelina Jolie.* I felt that all-too-usual mouth-watering that was a part of my battle. I was *not* going to lose this one.

I can do this, I thought. *I've got this!*

The battle did not wage long. Having been duped by these emails before, I knew that the pics were not of Angelina Jolie, but I've always had a bit of a celebrity crush on her, so I took the chance.

I was right. It wasn't her.

But that simple *click* led me to an unusual site that promised *Naughty Schoolgirls.* Not wanting to seem pervish, but I will admit that I found Brittany Spears' music video "Hit Me Baby One More Time" oddly scintillating, so I forged ahead.

As usual, one site led to another led to another. Time seemed to suck into a vortex. Before I knew it, I could hear the rattle of my wife's keys in the front door.

5

During my lunch break at work, I stole away to a local adult shop to take a gander around. I parked in the rear of the building and hoped that I could sneak into the front door in the shadows. I don't know why I thought I could walk in the front door as easily as a grocery store. I did my best spy moves for fear that someone from work, or worse, someone from church might see me.

Certain I had escaped notice, I wanted to go behind the curtain. I could discern the voice of The Great and Powerful Oz, *Pay no attention to the man behind the curtain.* I was, at least for today, no Cowardly Lion. I was going in. I felt as out of place as Goldilocks breaking into and entering the three bears' house.

What appeared before me was a long hallway of closed doors. The familiar sounds of bad music and moans could be heard from behind the doors. I didn't understand the rules governing behavior, so I must have missed the signs reading "Occupied" and suddenly interrupted a bespectacled man who clearly was enjoying his time in the booth. Mortified, I excused myself and begged pardon for the gaffe.

I found an empty stall and entered the little cave. Before me was a small TV screen. Previews of available offerings appeared on the screen begging me to choose. An action sequence I found interesting caused me to get over my skeeviness. If what I had interrupted moments before happened regularly in this room, I worried about touching anything or getting touched by something. The overall concern abated as I got comfortable with the sequences occurring onscreen.

Oddly enough, I would never pay for porn on the computer; I couldn't risk a credit card trail. But here in this little booth, it was nothing for me to slip multiple dollars in the slot. By the time break was over, I had gone through virtually everything I had in my wallet. And I hadn't eaten yet.

I went back to work feeling shamed and disgusting. I felt dirty. I won't even mention how I smelled. The stench of stale cigarettes permeated every stitch of my clothing. When I got home that afternoon, the first thing my wife asked, "Why do you smell like smoke? You smoking now?"

"I was hanging outside with all the smokers. We were talking about something important—an upcoming project."

"Y'all couldn't get a meeting room?"

I had picked up a few extra hours working part-time at the post office to supplement my income from the church. My youth pastor's salary was laughable. *How can they expect anyone to live on that?*

"I feel bad for the smokers. Everywhere they go they are pushed out or shunned. It's sad to see them huddled at the entrance to the door. I can't imagine being so hooked on anything like those poor suckers."

I really never understood smoking. Why would anyone ignore the Surgeon General's warning? It may as well read, *"If You Smoke This, You Will Die!"*

"Well, then, go take a shower. You stink."

In the shower, I chuckled a little. I could not believe I had gotten away with such a ridiculous lie. I mean, how gullible could she be?

I scrubbed and scrubbed, but I couldn't wash the shame away—no matter how hard I tried or how much shampoo I used. I remembered the song we used to sing years ago:

> *What can wash away my sins,*
> *Nothing but the blood of Jesus.*

I loudly let a few bars go. I did my best singing in the shower. I felt good as I sang; I could feel myself drawing closer to God. In the shower I didn't have to be ashamed to let a few tears fall. I wondered, *How did I get to this point? How'd it get so bad? I don't want to be like this anymore.* I pleaded in prayer, "God, please help me! I can't do it without you. I don't want to live like this. This thing is controlling me."

I promised God that I would never do it again. I was going to clean up my act. I had been going in circles, searching for old spiritual landmarks, trying to find my rightful place. I had somehow gotten on what I call the cycle of sin. You know it—sin, *Lord forgive me*—sin, Lord forgive me—sin, *Lord forgive me*...with no change in behavior. It's like riding a stationary bike. You pedal and pedal but go nowhere. I know asking for forgiveness is an essential element, but I also knew that true repentance meant turning from doing the same old things.

I constantly worried about having a reprobate mind. There is a conscience-searing that takes place when you repeatedly sin. Searing a piece of meat when cooking locks the juices inside and locks everything else out. Most good cooks know that when a steak is fully seared, it will easily release from the pan. How did I expect to continue to return to the place of my greatest sickness and failure, and still have victory? Maybe I was going crazy. As Einstein decreed—insanity is doing the same thing over and over again and expecting a different result. Jesus himself spoke about the dog returning to its own vomit.

Numerous times I had sat before my computer in my *I hate myself position*, still rationalizing that I was a good Christian, that I was going to make a good pastor. Sadly, I maintained that I was an effective spiritual leader thinking that I could provide solid Christian counsel to those who needed pointing in the right direction.

I even argued with myself that doing this would make me a better leader. How was I supposed to help someone else struggling with porn addiction if I did experience porn for myself? I believed that understanding the darkness was essential to helping someone find the light—or at least that was my rationale.

Sitting in church on Sundays was a task; the devil would remind me over and over again how bad I was. I replayed my bad behavior and habit in my head. I admitted to impure thoughts as I watched my fellow female congregants parade to the offering basket. I wondered if they could do some of the exploits I had seen on the computer screen.

Time and again I wondered if I could break free from the temptation. That would take me deeper on a study of where temptations come from. I'm a word guy, but sadly, sometimes the English language is faulty. We have only one word for temptation. We think about it as an enticement to sin, but you could also be tempted to do what's right. Famed pastor Bishop T.D. Jakes once asserted that all sin and problems in human relationships can be traced to the lust of the flesh, the lust of the eyes, and the pride of life.

The lust of the flesh includes a drawing towards impure desires, sinful pleasures, and sensual gratification. Because many people interpret lust as simply related to sexual pursuits, it is important to note that sensual gratification refers to being preoccupied by and indulging appetites of all kinds—what can be seen, heard, smelled, touched, and tasted.

The lust of the eyes refers to coveting or desiring those things which are attractive to the eye but forbidden by God, including the desire to watch that which gives sinful pleasure. Much of what we view and hear in the mass media today is spiritually harmful to us. I was not careful, so I had been sucked in by the world's *entertainment* of pornography, violence, ungodliness, and immorality. Moses' instructions about coveting certainly coincide with this teaching—desiring what someone else has can quickly lead us astray.

I imagined being like Eve in the Garden of Eden. When the serpent came to Eve in the Genesis account, he used these lusts to his advantage. Eve must have been hungry at the time because his first appeal was to her flesh. God had granted the first couple the ability to eat from any tree in the garden except one, the tree of the knowledge of good and evil. Perhaps she was standing in the garden trying to figure out which of the bountiful blessings she would partake. Maybe her eyes flickered from tree to tree as she tried to make a decision. Capitalizing on her physical hunger, the serpent spoke directly to her sensual lust—*Eat the fruit and you will be satisfied.*

Secondly, he appealed to the lust of the eyes. Standing there in the midst of the Lord's handmade orchard, the fruit of this particular tree must have had that special *ting* from the toothpaste commercials. The serpent told her to ignore God's promise of death. *You won't die,* he said. *In fact, if you eat the fruit, your eyes will be opened. You'll see the world differently; You'll really know what's going on.* The scriptures indicate that Eve *saw that the tree was good for food, and that it was pleasant to the eyes.*

Finally Satan delivered the blow that is still being heard around the world; he hit her with the pride of life. *You'll be just like God—knowing all, seeing all—if you just eat the fruit.* She succumbed to the desire to make herself wise, to be a know it all. In that moment, the idyllic state changed to our present reality.

I guess the old adage is true. Ignorance is bliss.

6

Six weeks later, it was my turn to preach the Sunday sermon. The other ministers and I were on a rotating preaching calendar. I wanted—no, I needed to make a good impression this time, so I studied my butt off making sure that I had biblical support for every thought.

On Sunday morning, Camille noticed that I was more nervous than usual. She inquired, "What's going on with you? Why do you seem so weird?"

"I'm just really nervous today. I'm ready to speak, but I feel uneasy."

"Just remember our agreement. Don't mention anything about me."

"I'm not gonna talk about you."

"Let me see your notes then," she challenged.

"You don't need to see my notes. I told you, I'm not going to even bring you up."

"Pardon me if I don't quite trust you to keep your word on that. Sometimes things just come to you. You have a tendency to go off-book."

"Then, I guess seeing my notes won't prove anything, will it? It's not that I care if you see my notes; I just don't like the idea of getting your permission to do my job or the insinuation that you need to fact check me. Besides, I've got sixty-six books of the Bible to preach from. I don't need to talk about us, I can talk about Jesus."

"Whatever. We'll see how it goes. But we gotta get to church; I'm going to be late for Sunday School class."

Not gonna lie, I was petrified during the worship service while I waited to be called up. Camille was right. I do go off on tangents. My last message's revelation was *out of the blue* as I had not planned to share what I did. Today I would be more careful. I was going to follow line by line, precept by precept. I had to. My chosen approach was a little *avant garde* anyway. Who knows how the congregation would receive me or my sermon.

Pastor Craft said a few words of welcome and greeting and asked the congregation to greet each other. He was really big on creating a community within the church.

He especially encouraged us to be on the lookout for faces we did not recognize. He wanted the visitors to feel loved and welcomed so they would come back. He really did not want to embarrass any of our guests. He just wanted to make them feel like they mattered. Some days, he would ask members to introduce the new people they'd met and tell the congregation a few facts about their new acquaintances.

"Pastor Bobby J, come on up and give us that *Good Word*."

I took a deep breath, grabbed my Bible and notes and took the steps to the rostrum.

"Thank you, Pastor Craft. I am always honored to grace this sacred desk and share with the people. I have a unique message today, and I'm anxious to see what y'all think."

I could feel the tangential tugging at my mind, and, as usual, I was too weak to resist.

"Before I begin, I feel the need to apologize to everyone. The last time I was up here, I laid a bombshell on you. I revealed my deepest secret, my struggle. I would love to stand here and say that I have overcome, but honestly, that would be a lie. It hasn't been easy, but I'm doing better. And I'm on my way. I do covet your prayers and support. Let us pray.

"Heavenly Father, full of compassion and forgiveness, please cover me with your grace and anointing. Take me and hide me behind the cross. Let them see me but hear you. Let the words of my mouth and the meditations of my heart be acceptable in thy sight, O Lord, My strength and My Redeemer. Amen."

"As I stated, my message today is a little unconventional, and I beg your indulgence as I take you back a little bit. I am using a familiar parable for my text today. You probably have heard this story a thousand times, but if your heart is open to it, you may hear something new this time. I'm not gonna ask you to turn to Matthew, Mark, Luke, or John, at least not yet, but I'm going to turn in the book of the Brothers Grimm to *Goldilocks and the Three Bears.*"

A few chuckles rippled through the crowd. "You may imagine this as merely a fictional children's story, but significant spiritual truths emerge as we explore the process of what I'm calling *sintimacy*. To help you remember the original story as told by the Brothers Grimm, my plan is to read verbatim from the text. I will then explicate the story using Goldilocks as a Christian and the common mistakes we make after coming to the Lord. I'm titling my message today, "Sintimacy: The Christian's Love Affair with Secret Sin."

I shared how I had been impacted by *good* television shows like *Sesame Street, Mister Rogers' Neighborhood, Zoom, Captain Kangaroo,* and *Romper Room*—educational programs on public television. One of my favorites was *The Electric Company.* On each episode, there was a phonics lesson where two silhouettes would pronounce a word phonetically. The shadowy figures would face one another, and one would say the first letter sound and the other the second. They would then pronounce the whole word together. For example: —b...at...bat or —c...at...cat.

"That's how I came up with the term, sintimacy. The word is made by compounding the words sin and intimacy. Let's take some time to explain both of these terms."

I explained how sin at its basic definition is missing the mark of righteousness that God sets for His people. Scriptures declare that our footsteps are ordered by God, and He expects us to follow after the Spirit.

"Any time we step outside of those borders is sin. To follow after our fleshly desires is sin. In archery, the goal is to hit the bullseye at the center of the target. Such is our directive from God—to walk in the *center* of his will. Unfortunately, many Christians are satisfied or even prefer to walk on the periphery of righteousness. They may live with the thought of, How *much sin can I get away with and still make it to heaven?*"

Continuing I added, "Many would argue, I suppose, that they

are not making this decision consciously. The rules of geometry dictate that the shortest distance between two points is a straight line. Hmmm. How might this be true in the rules of living holy?

"Sin, at various times throughout the scriptures, is also denoted as transgression, wrongdoing, wickedness, injustice, failure to love—*let that one sink in for a moment*—defiance of the law of God, and finally, an enslaving and deceiving power.

"This last one will be my focus today. From these definitions, we can conclude that the essence of sin is selfishness—a grasping of things or pleasures for ourselves, regardless of the welfare of others and the commandments of God. Ultimately sin becomes the refusal to be subject to God and His word. The manifestations of sin are myriad, but Jesus spoke to the types of sin, or what he described as *those things that defile*. Let's read Mark 7:20–23."

I paused while parishioners flipped pages. Taking up the text, I read:

> *"And he said, That which cometh out of the man, that defileth the man. For from within, out of the heart of men, proceed evil thoughts, adulteries, fornications, murders, Thefts, covetousness, wickedness, deceit, lasciviousness, an evil eye, blasphemy, pride, foolishness: All these evil things come from within, and defile the man."*

I stepped down from the stage, as was my custom when I wanted to emphasize a point. I began to walk down the center aisle. I had always fancied myself a man of the people, so I wanted to get face to face with the common folk. I talked as I walked.

"Giving in to the power of sin, for the Christian, is supposed to be a non-issue. Numerous scriptures indicate that once we come to Christ, we have power over sin; are dead to sin; have been raised to new life; and are no longer servants to sin. Yet, everywhere we turn, Christians are falling under its spell. I've deduced the main reason—we make excuses so that we can do whatever we want. Excuses for giving in to sin are many; three of the most popular are:

"I'm only human.

"The devil made me do it.

"Nobody's perfect.

"Raise your hand if you've ever spoken those words."

There was some reluctant but honest few.

"Most of the excuses we give are meant to shift the blame and responsibility to someone other than—me. The problem with these excuses is that the Bible contradicts them all. God has made us —new. Old things are passed away; we have been given authority and power to resist the devil; and through his strength we are made perfect. The reality is, however, that many of us Christians have lost sight of the target—the mark for the prize of the *high* calling of God and at the same time have confused God's grace and mercy for weakness or stupidity. What we forget is God's high expectations for righteousness. We forget the Biblical examples of failure and its consequences."

To an outsider watching, my walking may have seemed aimless or pointless. My public speaking professor often told the class to make movements purposeful. My movements were intentional, so I could observe the crowd. The faint crackling of a candy wrapper drew my attention toward Sister Cynthia who quietly shoved a butterscotch candy from her purse into the open mouth of her grandbaby. *She's trying to be so slick.* My mom used to do the same thing to me with those striped peppermints or those little red-wrapped strawberry hard candies. Hers were always covered with purse lint though.

"Remember the story of Adam and Eve? God's handmade creations were given the entire Garden of Eden to govern, and in a split second, lost it all—for simply eating a piece of fruit. Moses, the only person to have a face-to-face meeting with God, was forbidden to enter the land of promise because he hit a rock with a stick. King Saul did *not* kill someone, and he and his descendants lost the kingdom forever."

Just then, Francheska's baby spilled his Tupperware canister of dry Cheerios. *She better clean that up or the janitor will be mad.* I recalled how the deacons and senior mothers would scowl at the idea of young women having food for their babies in the sanctuary.

I looked around and blistered at the number of young children with electronic screens in their faces. When I was younger, I had to be a *good boy* to get my mom to give me a pen just so I could draw on the back of the church bulletin.

I continued, "These individual acts of disobedience brought God's wrath—how do you think He feels about His children who continually live in secret sin?"

I stepped back onto the stage. "Whoo, it's hot up here!" Feeling parched, I guzzled from the glass of water the ushers had prepared for me and shed my suit jacket before continuing. For sure, pit stains of sweat had soaked my checked blue shirt. I wiped my brow with a towel.

"Our natural, fleshly inclination is to hide our sins. *Both* Adam and Cain had secret sins. Adam, in his shame, sewed fig leaves together to hide his nakedness. When the Lord found him and Eve, they were hiding among the trees in the garden. This is the problem of living in sin. The shame and guilt cause us to shun God. We are afraid and uncomfortable in His presence—rightfully fearful of His glory.

"When we are in sin, we feel it is impossible to draw near to him with confidence; we run *from* him instead of *to* him for deliverance. Like Adam and Eve, our sinful conditions cause us to retreat from the presence of God, despite the scriptural urging to *boldly approach the throne of grace, that we may obtain mercy.*

"You know when we need mercy? When we've done something wrong."

A chorus of *Amens* echoed in the chamber. I smiled as I recognized my words were punching the right buttons.

"Cain murdered his brother and then buried Abel's body under the ground." I tried to make my point firmly. "When confronted by God, Cain did what most of us do—act like we didn't know it was wrong. He pretended like he hadn't seen Abel. Christians do this quite well—they say—it was just a mistake; I couldn't help it; it was someone else's fault; I was pressured into doing it; everyone's doing it.

"Someone once said, *Excuses are monuments to nothing, built on a bridge to nowhere.* God cursed Cain for his hidden sin, and instead of responding with repentance, Cain separated himself from God and decided to live as a *fugitive and a vagabond* as it says in Genesis 4:14. There is a danger in unrepentant sin and the hubris it creates in our own hearts.

"Let me get to back the story."

I pick up the book and I read.

"The story of *Goldilocks and the Three Bears* begins in a very large forest near a small village. A quaint cottage rests at the edge of the forest and there dwells three bears—Mama Bear, Papa Bear, and Baby Bear. They live a very peaceful life there and rarely have visitors.

"One day Mama Bear made the family breakfast, a delicious porridge. Upon tasting the porridge Mama Bear found it far too hot for the family to eat, so she suggested they take a walk while it cools and eat it upon their return. Papa Bear grabbed his hat and Mama her bonnet and together with Baby Bear off they went into the woods.

"Shortly after they leave, a young girl, Goldilocks, wanders past their cottage. She is quite tired and hungry from walking through the woods and stops at the bears' house."

A child's voice rang out from the congregation, "Ooh, I love this story."

"And I do, too. It's one of my favorites," I shot back to the kid. Several chuckled at my response. I kept going.

"We find Goldilocks traipsing through the woods. She ends up in a bears' house eating up all their food. At some point, she sits in their rocking chairs, leans back, and then *boom*; the chair breaks. The story makes this point, *Goldilocks is stunned and still tired, so she brushes herself off and goes upstairs to see what's there.*

"Wait a minute," I interrupted myself. "She's in a bear's house. I mean, she doesn't necessarily know it's a bear house, but she knows it ain't *her* house. She done ate all their food, and now she done broke the furniture. Take the hint, Goldilocks. For heaven's sakes! I'll never understand this next part. She was so tired, so she went upstairs to bed."

I pantomimed confusion. People laughed.

"She finds herself at the top of the stairs looking into the bears' bedroom. She saw a large bed, a medium bed, and a little, itty bitty bed. The larger mattresses didn't fit her fancy—too hard, too soft, but then that baby mattress—ahhh, just right. Soon, she's asleep."

"After a period of time, the Bear family returns to find the door open, the porridge sampled, chair shattered, and upon searching, a sleeping little white girl in the baby's bed. When she heard the baby bear's voice of surprise, Goldilocks jumped up in fear and ran home.

"Now, you tell me what happened next. How do these stories end?"

The crowd shouted, "Happily ever after."

"Let me ask you, where did Goldilocks go wrong in her Christian walk? How is she a sintimate Christian? Her experiences in the wilderness are very telling."

I detailed each point.

"One—She entered a strange land.

"Two—She walked deeper into the wilderness.

"Three—She did something she would not ordinarily do.

"Four—She opened the door of a stranger's house.

"Five—She took a good whiff.

"Six—She took a taste.

"Seven—She asked, *How much can I get away with?*

"Eight—She got the "–itis." I charade the air quotes. "Maybe Goldilocks was black after all?" Numerous chuckles around the room.

"Nine—She got comfortable in a stranger's house.

"Ten—She ignored the wake-up call.

"Eleven—She went even deeper into the house.

"And number twelve—She fell asleep.

"Goldilocks' first problem was being out in the woods alone. For the life of me, I can't figure out why, in all of these types of fairy tales, these little girls are out in the wilderness by themselves. The characters in the stories are most often children—Goldilocks, Little Red Riding Hood, Hansel and Gretel, etc. If we look at the imagery related to the definition of a wilderness: an unsettled, uncultivated region left in its natural condition, a large wild tract of land covered with dense vegetation or forests; an area that is barren or empty; a waste; or a piece of land set aside to grow wild. Goldilocks ain't had no business out in the wilderness! Can I get an Amen?"

I could tell I had struck a chord by the numbers of *Amens* I heard.

I continued, "And if we look at this definition from a biblical/spiritual perspective, the wilderness is not a place for Christians to be hanging out either. The dark place is not the right element for children of light. The Bible says that light and dark cannot share the same space."

To call attention to the likes of Sister Jean, I stepped off the podium and went to stand near her.

"There are people here who no doubt understand how Goldilocks may have felt. She's out in the wilderness and recognizes that she is tired and a little bit hungry; being in the wilderness can do that—make you tired and make you seek out things that will get your need met, because typically when we are dealing with the issues of sintimacy, the tough stuff that has been temptations and struggles for us—when we're in the dark place, we begin to seek out those things."

"I know that's right!" Sister Jean was probably flashing back to the times she had been chasing down a crack rock before the Lord found her. She leaned to her side and high fived Sister Sharon. They both shared the same testimony of deliverance. The long feathers protruding from her church hat trembled in agreement.

"When we're living in the wilderness, the hunger intensifies, and when the hunger intensifies, the *I gottas* get stronger." I surmised by the bobbing heads, I was talking right, so I continued.

"You must understand that Goldilocks was from a good home. How do we know this? She had golden locks. Think about the pictures you've seen; she is well-kempt. In the old stories and movies, the mean and evil people wore black, but not our heroine. She was well-dressed and her hair was maintained. She came from a good home; she had some good *home training* as they say. Doesn't it seem odd that a young girl from a good home is out in the woods by herself?"

"Sure does, Pastor. Preach on!"

"As she is wandering through the woods, she comes upon a house. Maybe it's the only house out there, and she realizes that she has traveled too far. Nevertheless, she knocks on the door, but no one is home. It seems to me, though, that someone with a modicum of home training who knocked on a door and got no response, wouldn't just walk into someone else's house—even if the door was unlocked."

"True!" The feminine voice came from the back on the left side.

"I am sure that at some point, Goldilocks' parents taught her that it was inappropriate to commit breaking and entering. I wonder how many strange houses Christians are walking into—even if the doors are open. That's the problem of sintimacy—when we get out into the wilderness, we do things that we would not ordinarily do, even things we have been instructed *not* to do."

I noticed the time on the clock on the back wall. *I had better bring this to a close.*

"Sintimacy permitted Goldilocks to take the extra step of turning the doorknob to enter the house of a stranger, somewhere in the middle of the wilderness. Remember now, the stranger was not even home; she was entering the home uninvited—maybe just for a little peek."

I cautioned the parishioners how sintimacy often operates in secrecy.

"I guarantee you that Goldilocks did not proudly announce her arrival into the strange house. I imagine that she looked over her shoulder a couple of times; before she tiptoed in the house. She peeked in; she did not just burst through the door."

I pantomimed how Goldilocks might had sneaked in the door.

"Why sneak? Because she knew she was in the wrong. Remember, she was not visiting her friend's house; she was not delivering a picnic basket to Grandma's house. She was in the woods breaking into the home of a complete stranger."

I lowered my tone for effect as I stressed my final point. "Friend, if you have to sneak or peek over your shoulder to see who's watching, chances are you are walking into a sintimate situation. Chances are that the activity is something you are not supposed to be doing."

"Preach, preacha!" Deacon Pettigrew's outburst signaled his agreement.

"When we live in sintimacy, sometimes we get into these quandaries about whether or not something is wrong. If you have to think about it, it's probably better—and safer—to err on the side of caution and not do it. Trust me; it will save you a whole lot of trouble."

I looked up as Pastor Craft returned to his seat. I hadn't even noticed he had walked out. Internally, I smiled as I imagined he trusted me to be able to deliver the message without fear I would say something that would have his phone ringing off the hook.

"Goldilocks gets into the house. Outside the house, there was still a chance to back out. There was a way of escape. Before she entered the strange place, she could have remembered that she was out of her element, that she had a home where she could be safe, well fed, and rested. Let me caution you to remember Ted Haggard's words: *Sin will take your farther than you want to go; it will cost you more than you want to pay. It will keep you longer than you want to stay.*"

I related the process of how sintimacy took her into the house, and here she is now, alone in the strange place. As was common— the hunger intensifies.

"If you've been sintimate, you probably understand being in the wilderness, in strange place and feeling your hunger intensify and your stomach start growling. How you experience the growling may be different, depending upon the sintimacy, but as the hunger intensifies, there's a signal that goes off in our brains that requires satisfaction. See, you must understand that when you repeatedly yield to sin's attempts at dominance, you are elevating that thing to the place of authority or godship in your life, because it has control over you."

With another swipe of the towel, I began my descent towards conclusion. I questioned, "Do you remember the reason why Goldilocks entered the house? She was hungry and in search of food. Surprise, surprise—she's in the house, and her eyes behold not one bowl of porridge, but three. They just magically appeared—she picked the right stranger's house to get her need met. The sintimate would see this phenomenon as a blessing from the Lord— *I was hungry and look at that—there's food on the table. He is Jehovah Jireh! God opened this door for me!* "Fool, you are out in the wilderness in a strange land. The Lord did not open the door for you and provide this meal."

Hands clapped. A few people stood up to express their accord.

"Sintimacy lulls us into misconstrued thinking that God will justify our position in the dark place because *He's going to use me here.* I have heard from teens who tell me that even though their friends are hanging out and doing drugs or drinking, that does not necessarily mean that they will too. In fact, they say that they're hanging out there with them to win them to the Lord, being a good Christian witness. If you are shaking your head right now, then you probably know that this type of thinking is faulty. Do I mean that Christians can't handle being around those who smoke, or drink or fill in the blank? Can't we win them there? All I am saying is that I am crazy enough to believe if God wants to save someone who is lost in that particular dark place, and he wants me to win them, then his spirit will draw that person out of the house and down the path to where I am so that I don't have to go into the wilderness to possibly get trapped. Amen?"

A few people answered the call and shouted back to me. I heard a couple "Amen brothers" and a "Preach on" or two, so I knew I was talking right.

"Don't get me wrong; I do believe that God will send certain people *into* the wilderness to rescue someone who needs deliverance, but I find it interesting that in the Gospel of St. Mark, chapter eight, Jesus, himself, had to remove a blind man from the cursed place of Bethsaida in order to perform the miracle." I paused before adding, "I'll save that for another sermon."

"So, it seems to me, that at times it is appropriate for a Christian to go, *with* the Spirit's leading and empowerment, into the dark place, but certainly not to go and hang out. Most likely, though, if you are struggling with a particular sin, the Lord is not going to require you to go to the place of your struggle to win someone, because it's a trap. It would be too easy for such a person to go in and get caught in the quicksand. It could be argued that Jesus called his disciples to be fishermen, not hunters. Fishermen use bait and cast a line out to draw the fish to them."

Agreeing with myself, I used a singsong, "*Well.*"

"Goldilocks stood looking at the bowls of porridge and decided to take a taste. The first bowl was—too hot. There are certain activities that a Christian will look at and say—*absolutely not*. That particular action is not tempting at all; that's too hot. But watch how sintimacy works; she went to the next bowl, and it was too cold. Again, certain activities are not attractive or tempting. She made one more try and found the bowl of porridge that was just right and sat down for a feast. This is a classic example of what my former pastor, Rev. Eric Brooks called, *greasy grace and sloppy agape*. The sintimate will keep trying certain activities—knowing that they are wrong—until they find one that is either easy to keep hidden or one easy to justify."

"After eating to her sintimacy's content, or maybe until the bowl was empty, Goldilocks got very sleepy. My friends call this the *-itis,* a medical condition where people start falling asleep soon after a meal. I believe the real medical condition is called reactive hypoglycemia. Immediately after having found the sintimacy that was just right, she got sleepy."

"I'm running out of time, but watch how sintimacy works. She was in the house of a stranger deep in the wilderness; she has eaten a tempting meal that was prepared *for* someone else—but somehow just right for her—and now, instead of leaving—you must remember that the food on the table was waiting for the inhabitants of the house to return—she goes and sits down in a chair next to the fire. She tries out several different chairs, looking for the one that is just right. In real estate, they say it's all about location, right? For Goldilocks, the just right chair was located next to the fire. This should have been another warning sign. Do take note also that each time, she found her *just right* in the baby bear's place. Scriptures record that it is the *little* foxes that destroy the vine. The sintimate often try the *little* things because they think that the *little* temptations and activities are safe.

"While taking her little siesta in the comfy chair, the chair breaks; but still that does not wake her up. She would prefer to stay comfortably resting in a stranger's house in the dark wilderness, where the owners of the house would be returning soon. A sintimate Christian begins to prefer the comfort of the darkness. The broken chair was a sign from the Lord to wake up and take notice of the location where she was standing."

I reminded them of the story of the prodigal son—how the lost boy found himself in a pigsty.

"The scripture declared that *he came to himself.* In other words, he took stock of his location and realized what his life had come to be. It was then that he decided to return home—but not our Goldilocks. You would think that after eating someone else's food and destroying their property, Goldilocks would get out of the house. But sintimacy had her so tired that she ignored the wake-up call.

"Sintimacy sent her upstairs to lay down. I watch a lot of the crime dramas on TV. Have you ever noticed that when the criminals are trying to escape the police officer's grasp, they almost always run upstairs towards the roof? Going deeper into the building is no way to escape; in fact, it almost always ensures their capture or eventual, accidental death."

"Once upstairs, Goldilocks was met with the same three choices as before—beds that are too hard, too soft, or just right. She chose the comfy baby bed, and the story tells us that she fell dead asleep— so asleep that she didn't know that the bears had returned home and were searching for the individual who entered their territory, eaten their food, and destroyed their property. Watch how your soul's enemy works; he follows your tracks. He likes it when we take his food because, like stray cats, if we take the bait once, it is difficult to get rid of us."

A male voice near the front shouted in agreement, "Say that!"

"The bears find Goldilocks asleep. Interestingly enough, it is the voice of the baby bear that awakens the sleeping girl. Goldilocks jumps out of the bed and tries to run away from the little bitty bear, but what she does not realize is that the baby is flanked by two larger bears. You have to understand that even though we are messing around with the little baby bears in our lives, when you get into a place of no escape with sin, that little one has some big friends. And now that we have realized that we have been in this place—tasting and trying what was *just right* and comfortable—there are hungry bears ready to pounce on the sleeping sintimate Christian.

"I know I've said it before, but I'm really coming to a close now."

A few people looked at their watches.

"Note that the bears could have found Goldilocks and said nothing—just started ripping her to shreds. They would have been well within their rights to do so. Goldilocks was in their home, had eaten their food, had broken their chair, and was now fast asleep in their private bedroom. The bears' natural instinct would have been to eat her; just as the devil's job is to *steal, kill, and destroy*. Yet, despite all of this, the grace and mercy of God was in action. Even though she was in the wrong place, had done many of the wrong things, and had fallen spiritually asleep, it was the grace of God that allowed Goldilocks to hear the little bear's voice. Even though she ignored the earlier warning of the broken chair, he awakened her from a deep sleep—*with a still, small voice*."

I noted a few tears running down some faces.

"The mercy of God allowed her to escape the clutches of three angry bears and to get out of the house in the wilderness."

I concluded with the caution how the grace that God provides—God's plan of escape—is given long before we get into the wilderness.

"Often we do not listen and willingly go into the stranger's house to try the stranger's wares, yet somehow he allows us to escape judgment and destruction. Ain't God good?"

I invited the congregation to stand to signal I had finally come to the end. I had not planned to speak that long.

"As we close today, perhaps there is one in the room who has had a Goldilocks experience, and you're tired of eating porridge that wasn't poured for you? Maybe you've fallen asleep in the bear's bed, and you are full of regret? Maybe you've whispered to yourself time and again how awful you are, and you've imagined that God's got a lightning bolt ready to strike you down? Friend, I know exactly how you feel. I know what it's like to be so heavy with guilt and shame. I've been on the bottom looking down still, but I want you to look up—not down—because there's a God with long, strong, outstretched arms ready to forgive you. He declares in Romans 8:1 that *There is therefore now no condemnation to them which are in*

Christ Jesus, who walk not after the flesh, but after the Spirit. God is not mad at you. King David recognized that God's *mercy endureth forever,* and that forever includes you—right here and right now. Receive his mercy today and be free of sintimacy. Pray my strength in the Lord."

With that, I took my seat while Pastor Craft invited congregants to repent at the altar. Afterwards, he gave the benediction.

I felt pretty good. That was until I saw Camille's face as I exited the room—her face filled with scorn and derision.

"What?" I questioned.

"I thought you weren't talking about us today."

"What are you talking about?"

"Sister Thelma interrupted my class and asked to speak with me. When I got into the hall, she hugged me and gushed about how brave and authentic you were, how we need that kind of honesty in the church." Gritting through her teeth, she leaned closer, "What did you say?"

"I did a lesson on how Goldilocks was an allegory and example of Christians who get caught up in sinful lifestyles. Nothing about you and nothing about me."

"What do you mean *nothing about you?* The last time you preached you told everybody that you are addicted to porn—don't you think they can add two and two and connect you to Goldilocks? Why are you so intent on embarrassing me every time you get up in front of the church? Everything you do or say reflects back to me! Now you'll have everybody thinking I'm not a good wife and don't take care of your *needs.*"

7

"**D**on't be so overdramatic. I didn't even mention your name. All I did was preach a sermon!"

"You think that's all you did. You embarrassed the *hell*, forgive me Jesus, in front of the whole Gee Dee church!" Her attempts at whispering didn't stop the onlookers.

Just then, Pastor Craft approached where we were standing. "Pastor Bobby, great message! Can I see you for a few moments in my office please?"

"Certainly, sir."

Seizing her *I-told-you-so* moment, Camille whisper-gloated, "See? Now you're going to get it."

I ignored her last comment. I sloughed it off mentally with, *Please, I'm a grown man.*

Upon entering his office, those chairs reminded me of my last *talking-to* where the pastor didn't rip me a new one—but probably should have. I quickly sat down to assume the position.

"Really good message. I love how creative you were. That is truly a gift. You made the Word understandable for the youngest person to the oldest person. No one is going to walk away confused today— that is, except me."

"I don't understand."

"You started off by admitting that you have struggled and have fallen short since last time, but I don't recall you reaching out to me like we agreed. If this accountability thing is going to work, you have to reach out. I may have the gift of prophecy, but I'm no mind reader."

Sheepishly, I admitted, "You're right, Pastor. I didn't call you, but I felt like I could handle it. Every time, I kept telling myself that I was stronger than the urge, that I didn't need to bother you."

"Your freedom is not a bother to me. I don't care how busy you think I am—that's what I'm here for! I wanna see you healed."

"But I really thought I had it this time. I can beat this thing."

"I-I-I! Remember what the Word says, *It's not by might, nor by power, but by my Spirit says the Lord.* You'll never be strong enough in and of yourself. You need God's help. As a man of God—let me help you."

"I'm so sorry Pastor. I was ashamed to call honestly."

"Well, I'll ask you like Jesus asked the man at the pool of Bethesda, *Do you want to get well?*"

"Of course, I do Pastor. More than anything."

"That's easy to say, but God's revelation of grace is what gives us the ability to act righteously. We typically speak of grace only as it relates to the expectation of blessing—God's unmerited favor. Grace is much, much more than that. It is an enabling power to do what is right, not an excuse to commit sin at will. You should consider grace an entry way into the will of God. Mercy, on the other hand, is protection from God's wrath. Do you have your Bible?"

I looked down at my Bible and notebook in my hand.

"Great. Turn to Romans." He began paging through the Bible he keeps on his desk. "Romans 2. Look how the Apostle Paul reveals the major problems with hidden lifestyles. Beginning at verse seventeen, Paul wrote:

"You who call yourselves Jews are relying on God's law, and you boast about your special relationship with him. You know what he wants; you know what is right because you have been taught his law. You are convinced that you are a guide for the blind and a light for people who are lost in darkness. You think you can instruct the ignorant and teach children the ways of God. For you are certain that God's law gives you complete knowledge and truth. Well then, if you teach others, why don't you teach yourself? You tell others not to steal, but do you steal? You say it is wrong to commit adultery, but do you commit adultery? You condemn idolatry, but do you use items stolen from pagan temples? You are so proud of knowing the law, but you dishonor God by breaking it.

No wonder the Scriptures say, 'The Gentiles blaspheme the name of God because of you.'"

Ooh, that one sat on me for a while. *Because of me. Because of my own sintimacy,* I thought, *there are scores of people who deny the existence of God, who revel in their presumption of the number of hypocrites in the church. Because of me the area of kingdom authority that I am supposed to have dominion over—my sphere of influence—was growing increasingly smaller. Because of me someone has refused the opportunity to get to know a loving, living Savior.* This fact was bothering me.

The Pastor's final words echoed in my mind, "We live this Christian life to impact others. Our lives are a letter written in our hearts; everyone can read it. So, if you are the only Bible that some will ever read—what facts of the saving power of Jesus Christ will they learn from your life? Even more importantly, what facts have you learned about the power of Jesus?"

✝✝✝

I only live a few miles from the church, but that was a long ride home! When things got quiet at home, for some reason, I pulled out a thesaurus and looked up the word "secret:"

covert stresses the fact of not being open or declared;

stealthy suggests taking pains to avoid being seen or heard especially in some misdoing;

clandestine implies secrecy usually for an evil, illicit, or unauthorized purpose and often emphasizes the fear of being discovered;

surreptitious applies to action or behavior done secretly often with skillful avoidance of detection and in violation of custom, law, or authority;

underhanded stresses fraud or deception.

On that last one, I closed the book. Each definition stabbed me like a dagger. I was living just like that! I wasn't letting myself off the hook, so I grabbed my concordance and my notebook and started to do some biblical word study to see what God had to say about secret sin.

By the time I completed my word search, I had, in total, over one hundred scriptures pronouncing God's displeasure with secret sin, but three really caught my attention. I wrote each one down in my notebook:

Luke 12:2–3: Jesus looks at secrecy as hypocrisy.

The time is coming when everything that is covered up will be revealed, and all that is secret will be made known to all. Whatever you have said in the dark will be heard in the light, and what you have whispered behind closed doors will be shouted from the housetops for all to hear!

Romans 2:6–9, 16: God's condemnation of secret sin.

He will judge everyone according to what they have done. He will give eternal life to those who keep on doing good, seeking after the glory and honor and immortality that God offers. But he will pour out his anger and wrath on those who live for themselves, who refuse to obey the truth and instead live lives of wickedness. There will be trouble and calamity for everyone who keeps on doing what is evil—for the Jew first and also for the Gentile. And this is the message I proclaim—that the day is coming when God, through Christ Jesus, will judge everyone's secret life.

Matthew 6:2–6: What happens in secret affects you publicly!

When you give to someone in need, don't do as the hypocrites do— blowing trumpets in the synagogues and streets to call attention to their acts of charity! I tell you the truth, they have received all the reward they will ever get. But when you give to someone in need, don't let your left hand know what your right hand is doing. Give your gifts in private, and your Father, who sees everything, will reward you. When you pray, don't be like the hypocrites who love to pray publicly on street corners and in the synagogues where everyone can see them. I tell you the truth, that is all the reward they will ever get. But when you pray, go away by yourself, shut the door behind you, and pray to your Father in private. Then your Father, who sees everything, will reward you.

What I had uncovered was that—*Nothing Is Secret!* I thought I was getting away with something, but these words only under-scored there is not much praise for secret behaviors in scripture; there is encouragement to find a secret place to be alone with God, but overwhelmingly Christians are called to living transparently so that we become a prism to reflect the wonder of Christ's glory.

Later that evening, I turned on the news. A story popped up about a presidential candidate I was a pretty big fan, so I paid attention. This person of high position was admitting to having an adulterous affair. I was shocked! He was reading a prepared personal statement:

"It is inadequate to say to the people who believed in me that I am sorry, as it is inadequate to say to the people who love me that I am sorry. In the course of several campaigns, I started to believe that I was special and became increasingly egocentric and narcissistic. If you want to beat me up—feel free."

I recalled how another preacher discussed his public fall from grace. He said something that stood out to me "We are only as sick as our secrets."

With that, I had come face-to-face with myself. I had taken a long hard look in the mirror, and frankly, did not like my reflection. I started to think hard on that. I was—*I am*—sick! When you are sick, one of the first thing you lose is your appetite. I had no real appetite for the things of God—my spiritual report card was marked *Needs Improvement.*

If Pastor Craft was right, and I suspected he was, my lack of spiritual skeleton was having an impact on others.

I thought, *If there is something wrong with my relationship with God, then my effectiveness as a witness for Jesus is severely limited. If I am a conduit for God's movement in the land, and my sin creates a barrier between me and God, then there is also a blockage between my sphere of influence and the presence of God.*

I needed to get right with God—at least that's what I was thinking. I also needed to get right with my wife. All those years of darkness blinded me to the *Ten Disciplines of a Godly Man.*

✝✝✝

We met for over an hour and barely scratched the surface of the first discipline—sexual purity. In that hour, we discussed the cultural bent towards sexuality and how men are not reared to admit fault. I stayed quiet for most of the discussion. I was afraid to admit my own fault. I wanted to be a pastoral authority. I looked around the room particularly at the men who were not saying anything—concerned as I was, fearing being called out—or that's what I surmised.

The pamphlet we were studying indicated sensuality as the "biggest obstacle to godliness" among Christian men. *Ain't that the truth?* It referenced King David's fall as a bit of a cautionary tale. As Pastor Craft suggested, it made studying and memorizing the scriptures a crucial piece. Brother Carlos, the leader of the group, began by reading 1 Thessalonians 4:3:

For this is the will of God, even your sanctification, that ye should abstain from fornication.

"See, it's the will of God. It's that serious. Too bad, many men discount this issue. You must view sensuality in its proper place—the will of God." He reemphasized, "Your body, according to 1 Corinthians 3, is *the temple of the Spirit.*"

This broke us off into much conversation. Brother Jason somehow took it to politics and government, but then Carlos mentioned transgenderism and the attempts to normalize such behavior. "Just wait," he confidently asserted. "Soon, they'll be making a legal argument in support of pedophilia."

When the subject turned toward how society handles youth sexuality, I saw that as an opportunity to insert my perspective. "A few years ago, I was taking my daughter clothes shopping, and we were walking through the department store, and they were selling thongs for three-year-old girls." Chagrined, I continued, "Honestly, my daughter was barely out of Pampers—a toddler mind you—and they're pushing thongs toward her." The men continued to carry on the conversation about how children are being exploited. That's when I interjected, "Parents unfortunately leave the conversation until it's too late. We don't address it until the kids are teenagers, and by then, they are ill-equipped for the all-out assault being waged for their souls. And the church is largely silent besides taking a sort of *don't ask, don't tell* policy. We don't have a healthy language to talk about sex other than to say, 'Don't do it.'"

Pastor Craft chimed in, "That's true. I can remember when I was younger, my Sunday School teacher Brother Edgecomb basically told us, 'If it brings you pleasure in any way it's a sin.' But speaking as a pastor, the church has tied my hands. I can't really address real issues like this in mixed intergenerational company on Sunday mornings. And that's pretty much all the time I get—about an hour a week."

That's when Brother Malcolm spoke up talking about how his life had changed once he surrendered to Christ. How his own love for his wife had changed, had deepened, now that he let Christ take control. Hearing this, I started thinking about Camille and how I felt like I was shortchanging her.

8

I lead youth group on Wednesday nights. That Wednesday, the youth leaders and I had planned a water balloon fight for the kids. The usual rule for events like this was *modest swimwear*. This was typically a rule of concern for the young ladies. *Modest* was a codeword for non-skimpy, one-piece bathing suits. Bikinis were traditionally forbidden; the general idea was that the girls were to dress as not to tempt the boys.

Rachel, however, did not get the message. She wore a plain white T-shirt over a black low-cut one-piece. The first balloon exploded on her back as she tried to run away. Clearly now—wet—she was not modest. The thin string of Lycra/Spandex revealed her buns of steel.

That girl is thick like a Snickers! In that wet T-shirt, her backside resembled two Honey Baked Hams.

She looked good.

I leaned over to Wendy, my volunteer youth leader, and drew her attention to the sight. Looking back on it, pointing it out was a ruse to give me more time to ogle without suspicion. I secretly thought about doing naughty things with this thirteen-year-old.

I hate everything about myself.

9

"**B**abe, I think I need help."

Admitting my struggle to her was the most terrifying thing I have ever had to do. "I can't seem to stop myself. It keeps calling me and calling me. I keep trying to leave it alone, but it seems like no matter what I try, nothing seems to be working." My thoughts about Rachel also scared me.

"I don't know how I can help you. Do you want to get one of those internet filter things? I read in the *Charisma* magazine about one porn filter that you can subscribe to that will send me a record of what websites you look at."

The prospect seemed far-fetched and a little condescending. I didn't want her to know everything I did online. It was a bit of a Catch-22. I thought back to those times when I was younger and had to hide out to do anything bad. *Look how far we've come as a society,* I thought. *Technology has changed everything.*

✝✝✝

I had gone to a church conference and heard a keynote address from Dr. Doug Weiss. In his talk, he referenced the real love man is supposed to have with his wife. He said, "The first time I saw my wife naked, I secretly said 'Behold the glory of God.'"

Weiss had shared that pornography, drugs—narcotics, over-the-counter, and prescription—and illicit and deviant sexual behavior are just a few of the ways in which some members of the body of Christ have been enslaved to sin. Committing sin seems so easy to us—especially since the advent of the internet. "All one has to do is punch a few keys, and they can have the world and all of its sinful pleasures within moments," Weiss warned. "We no longer have to contend with going to a house of ill repute—to the crack house or the whorehouse—to get our fix."

What a shame; it was the going that kept me out of those places. The fear of someone seeing me, getting caught, being asked, *Hey, I thought you were a Christian—what are you doing here?* was once enough to keep me on the straight-and-narrow. Not so anymore—I could have what I want and do what I want and never have to leave the house. I can have my sin mail ordered, and nobody ever had to know. Yet, *the eyes of the Lord are in every place, beholding the evil and the good!*

As long as my problem was secret and hidden, I was able to get away with it and for so long felt justified because, "I was not hurting anyone else but me." At the heart of this secrecy, to be honest, though, was the spiritual competition that we seem to have with other Christians. While I didn't want to portray a holier than thou attitude, and I rejected modern-day Phariseeism—that's exactly how I operated. I wanted to appear holy and righteous before others—the operative word being *appear*. My spiritual life was a mere facade that had been fabricated through attention to superficial details of clothing, language—*churchy talk*—and church attendance and participation. All the while, I was living, or dying, in secret darkness.

✝✝✝

"I just don't feel God anymore. It's like he's abandoned me, but I know he hasn't. He promised never to leave us or forsake us. Pastor Craft repeatedly questioned whether I had been reading my Bible. My Sunday School class memory verse we've been working on is Psalm 119: 9:

> *Wherewithal shall a young man cleanse his way? By taking heed thereto according to thy word.*

Camille retorted, "You know this, Bobby. Freedom only occurs with compliance and obedience to the Word of God. No simple force of willpower—although I must stress you have some level of personal responsibility here—no simple steps to walk through, and no magic bullets here. Strict adherence to the Word of God, following after his spirit and direction is the only clear path to true freedom in Christ. You need to be honest with yourself, with God, and with me."

After a few moments of awkward silence, Camille grabbed my hands and said, "Can I be really honest about something? I've been struggling too. Ever since you first admitted that you watch online porn; I have been doing the same thing."

"What? You have too?"

"I had to. I had to figure out the big attraction. I was curious to know what you were so wrapped up into. I was trying to keep up with the *competition*. I didn't know what else to do. Don't you find me attractive anymore?"

"Of course I do." My matter-of-fact tone seemed artificial.

"But you hardly ever watch to touch me anymore. I know I've put on weight since the baby was born, and these sites make me less confident that you find me desirable."

Now I really felt bad. "This is *my* problem, honey. I still love you as much as I did when we first got together."

"That doesn't answer my question," she waxed indignant. "I asked if you wanted me; if you find me desirable."

"Oh, baby…of course I want you! I love your body. I'm just as hot for you now as I was when we first got married! I don't know why I am so attracted to those websites. I've tried to guess at that; all I've really ever come up with is it seems like I've been missing something. I've been in the church for so long that maybe I felt like I didn't get to experience something. I remembered how I wanted to be like my brothers—they were having sex with everything with a slit."

"So you want to be like them, huh? Those man-whores? You wonder why I feel inadequate? That's why! When you admit your jealously of them, it makes me wonder why I'm not enough for you!"

I wanted to keep arguing, but no matter what I thought about saying, all of my arguments would lead us back to that statement. I couldn't think of a comeback, and I didn't want to see those tears of disappointment in her face anymore. She is my pillar of strength—the rock in our relationship, but I could tell that this conversation was eroding that confidence.

I also didn't want to have to keep apologizing for myself.

After several minutes of silence, she chimed in, "So, we're done talking about this?"

"I don't know what else to say. I'm damned if I do, and I'm damned if I don't."

If looks could kill. She glared at me with eyes pleading for answers that I didn't have—and couldn't conjure up.

Dissatisfied, she begged, "Talk to me!"

We used to be able to talk about anything. We used to be able to just look at each other and know what the other was thinking. We could finish each other's sentences or start singing a song that was only playing in the mind of the other. Telling my own wife about the depth of my addiction and the levels of depravity was one of the most difficult things I had to do. I had to stare into those eyes —which are my normal place of comfort and praise—only to reveal what I knew would cause tears. Sitting in my kitchen, not only did I have to confess my depravity, but in the interest of full disclosure, I had to tell her the numerous ways I had lied to her so I could do what I wanted to do.

I will never forget her face; not sadness, but a terribly angry pity. I had expected her to yell and rant at what a coward I had been, how I was a failure. Imagine my surprise when she shared feelings of inadequacy as a wife. She reported how my failures made her feel she had not been a good wife, how she must have failed me in some way. Imagine that—I was the one with the moral failures; I was the one who was committing sin and betraying her trust; but there she was blaming herself. She was admitting to me that my telling her about my addiction aroused a curiosity within her that would lead her down a similar path. What could I say?

With crocodile tears running down my cheeks, I strained, "I'm a failure. A failure as a minister and as a husband."

"No, you're not."

Ordinarily, I yearned for her to be my defense against the bad words I spoke about myself, but today the words seemed inadequate—as inadequate as I felt.

"Have you told your men's prayer group about this?"

The conversation ended without any real resolution.

I had told the men's group. I found it easy to confess to guys whom I knew struggled in the same area. That's what we do when we are not really serious about changing. You see, those guys would be able to empathize with my failures; they would pat me on the back and commence to share with me how they too had struggled or failed that week. Yes, in some convoluted way, I was being accountable to these men—I mean, I let them in on my dirty little secret. If I were honest with myself at that time, I probably would never have told them if I didn't already know that they struggled too.

I had set up fake accountability groups with them. These didn't help. Just because someone knows about the problem doesn't guarantee freedom. Oh, we would get together and pray about the struggle, but none of us would call each other at the moment of temptation—only after failing. The goal of accountability systems is protection from failure, not a pity party afterwards.

As Pastor Craft was suggesting I do with him, an accountability partner needs to be given access to your life, your thoughts; they should know your temptations and weaknesses. I needed to eliminate secrets; the best accountability systems are those where your partner can ask you any real question about your issue, and you would be completely frank and open.

10

Pastor Craft's sermonic text declared from Proverbs 24:16:

"For a just man falleth seven times, and riseth up again: but the wicked shall fall into mischief."

Introspectively, I questioned, *How can someone who has fallen so many times be declared just?*

By the time he read his New Testament scripture 2 Corinthians 5:17, *If any man be in Christ, he is a new creature: old things are passed away; behold all things are become new,* I questioned what it truly meant to be *in Christ.* And I wondered, I continue to struggle with a particular sin or problem, does this mean I am *not* in Christ?

✝✝✝

Rob Brendle, who took over Haggard's role as pastor, spoke about the Christian method of *sin management* which he described as the *whack-a-mole method* that described my life to a T. I was simply reactive to my bad acts—feeling guilty and sorry *after* the fact. I would cry and pray and make promises to God. Rather than looking deep inside for the root cause of *why* I was drawn to certain elements or activities; sin managers just wait until the bad acts pop up.

Following up on my wife's suggestions, I had downloaded one of those filtering programs on my laptop—not the one that would tell her what I had been up to, but one that I would control. They didn't work. At least as long as I had the password. When I wanted to usurp the accountability, I could punch in the right keystroke combination and there was my *prize.*

I played around with that program on my computer, but it got old real quick. Every time I got the urge—which was often—I had to go through the program, put the password in and then go online. It was a pain.

The months rolled by as I continued on my sin cycle. I felt bad, shameful, guilty, all the emotions each time I fell. I had the right tools but wasn't trying to use them properly. I kept praying. I went to bed with such guilt only to wake up with an, I *don't want to fall anymore* attitude.

My prayers sounded like this: "God, I'm so tired of living like this! Please help me!"

The Lord would speak back to me: "Do the first things first."

The book of Revelation speaks about repenting and doing the first works. This includes prayer and Bible study. How I avoided doing those things. After all these years, why was it so hard for me to pray? Read my Bible? I faithfully went to church, so I got my fill of the Word—heard preachers and teachers admonishing me to *seek God*. But I had been going to church all my life. Why was this such a foreign concept?

I sat in the den one afternoon, and I read in *Christianity Today* magazine about XXX Church. The article mentioned how they had been fighting porn addiction among Christians for nearly twenty years.

So I went to their website. There they indicated their mission:

It's time to stop blaming the porn industry for our problems. Legislation and pointing fingers doesn't work. Society and church culture continues to foster a "don't ask, don't tell" environment where we don't welcome these conversations because they are uncomfortable and challenging.

We need to shift culture so that anyone can pursue healing without fear of marginalization or being looked down upon. It's time to recognize that we all hurt and need help, and the only real difference is the type of pain we are dealing with.

XXXChurch is here to be that voice of change while providing places and resources needed to aid those struggling and in need of help today.

Then I read a powerful set of words written in bold print:

It's time for a change.

I've said it before. It had become a sort of mantra. I had become a broken record. But in that moment, I believed it. Today, I am committed. Sadly, the war was not over.

I read in Romans, Chapter 7, the Apostle Paul struggled with something. It probably wasn't porn, but something as sinister. He wrote in verses 15–25:

> *For that which I do I allow not: for what I would, that do I not; but what I hate, that do. If then I do that which I would not, I consent unto the law that it is good. Now then it is no more I that do it, but sin that dwelleth in me. For I know that in me (that is, in my flesh,) dwelleth no good thing: for to will is present with me; but how to perform that which is good I find not. For the good that I would I do not: but the evil which I would not, that I do. Now if I do that I would not, it is no more I that do it, but sin that dwelleth in me. I find then a law, that, when I would do good, evil is present with me. For I delight in the law of God after the inward man: But I see another law in my members, warring against the law of my mind, and bringing me into captivity to the law of sin which is in my members. O wretched man that I am! who shall deliver me from the body of this death? I thank God through Jesus Christ our Lord. So then with the mind I myself serve the law of God; but with the flesh the law of sin.*

Whenever I was home alone for a few hours, I had the fight of my life. I would think of different search terms to Google in hopes of getting the next thrill. I shocked myself with some of the phrases I typed in. I didn't ordinarily talk like that. Why was it so easy to type those words in that little box? Each search was a slightly more raunchy than the last freaky word.

So often I almost got caught as my attention was so focused on the screen that I missed the sound of the car pulling into the driveway. So many times I stupidly relied on the dog getting agitated when a car got near the house. I had gotten proficient at quickly closing windows on the laptop. I hated that I had grown proud of being duplicitous and sneaky. But deep down, I *was* sorry.

Even now, that voice says, "Yeah, you sure are—*sorry.*"

This morning, I knew I would have the house to myself. I woke up, and the beast was right there to greet me, calling me, beckoning me to go to the computer. *You've got at least three or four hours to yourself. You can do this with no worries.*

No, I'm better than that! I will not give in. I'm a vessel of honor. I had invoked the 1 Thessalonians 4 reminder that it was up to me to *possess* my vessel with sanctification and honor. I tried to be strong, but I think that was part of the problem. *I* was trying to do it. Each week, I responded to the altar call and invitation at church with a repentant heart—pledging I never would do this again. Believing that was the last time. I'd try to pray along as the pastor laid his hands on my head.

Sadly, that voice reminding me of my failures was louder than the pastor's. *What are you crying for? You know what you did last night. You know what you're going to do as soon as you get home.*

Tears of sorrow and shame quickly turned to tears of victimhood as I realized—the voice was right.

My next turn to preach was for an evening service. I decided the title of the sermon would be, "Walking in Limited Light." As I rose to the podium, I asked the ushers to turn off all the lights in the sanctuary.

Once it was dark, I asked the congregation to turn in their Bibles to the scriptural text for the day, and to read it aloud. Naturally, there were cries of, "We can't see," and "It's impossible to read this in the dark." I probably could have concluded the sermon right there—it is difficult to do the things of God, such as reading the Bible, while walking in darkness.

Yet and still, thousands of us try. Later, I turned on a lamp that I had on the platform so I could see my notes. The congregation remained in the dark, though my light helped them see a little. When the ushers turned the lights back on at the conclusion of my sermon, there were anguished cries of pain as people's eyes tried to readjust to the light. This is our exact response when God turns his light on our sinful lives—we want to retreat to the darkness where we were more comfortable. Talk about preaching to yourself. This was my life.

I don't know where I got so many fetishes. The things I was looking at were shocking. Each week was a little darker. Each time I went back, it was a little more disgusting. I managed to stay clean for a few weeks to a couple months, but the beast was always on my case. The monkey was definitely on my back.

The book of Luke talks about the struggle I was having. Jesus' disciples were wondering about demon possession and exorcism. Jesus told them that when an unclean spirit leaves a man it continues to search for a body to inhabit. If it doesn't find a new host, it returns to the place it had vacated. This time, he brings *seven other spirits more wicked than himself*. I imagined that each fall brought back seven more inhabitants.

Yes, I concluded. I am demon possessed.

I felt small, worthless, and ineffectual. I was not good. A failure. Rotten to the core. That's what I kept telling myself. I wish I could say that was the end, but I was up and down all the time. My spiritual life was like an economic graph—high mountains and deep valleys. I liked to pretend it was emotional turmoil in my life that caused me to lose the daily struggle. Nope, I did it because I liked it. Yet, I *didn't* like it.

One day, during a season of mountain highs, I was traveling down the highway with my wife. We drove past one of those adult shops I frequented in secret. "I'm just so glad God set me free from that life—from those places."

"I really wish you would quit saying that." Camille spoke with a deepness to her voice putting a serious quash on my praise.

"Why? I *am* thankful."

"Don't you understand how every time you say your thanks, it's a reminder of the ways I failed you as a wife? Of my shortcomings?" Tears rolled down her face.

"I never thought about it that way. I'm so sorry, babe." I drove with my head and heart down. It was a long ride. If I didn't feel shame before, I certainly felt it now. It got worse though.

"I think I told you that after you admitted your problem, I started watching the videos too. I wanted to know why you were so wrapped up..." I tried to interrupt her, but she cut me off. "I know you said it wasn't related to me, but I needed to know how I failed. I needed to know why I wasn't enough for you. I guess I got hooked too. Can you forgive me?"

How this woman loved me. Here she was asking for my forgiveness and at the same time telling me that my great failure created a stumbling block for her too.

"I guess I never thought about that." She had always been a pillar of moral, emotional, and spiritual strength. I couldn't begin to imagine her looking at some of the scenes I had.

"You need to call your brothers," Camille forcefully suggested.

I knew she wasn't talking about the boys I grew up with. After all, they were self-admitted man-whores. They never met a woman's body they didn't try to sleep with. She meant my prayer group. I used to attend a men's prayer group years ago. We met every Thursday evening at 10:00 after all the day's activities were done, kids were in bed. Just us. *Men.* I was never one to have a lot of male friends. I wasn't really interested in sports, so I never quite felt comfortable at men's gatherings. But, Thursday nights were the one place where I could be myself. I could let it all hang out—so to speak.

11

"Hey, Brent! It's been forever. How's it going?" I had called Brent when we got home. I stole away into the bedroom. I didn't even turn the lights on.

"Bruh! What's going on? It's great to hear from you." Brent's joviality felt authentic.

"Are you guys still meeting on Thursday nights? I think I need to see my brothers."

"We haven't really been meeting, but I'm sure I can get everyone together—if you need us."

"I do. It's pretty bad. Do you think we can make it happen this week?

"Say no more. I'll get on the phone right now. Even if we can't get everyone, I'm sure I can get the faithful few. We only need two or three to get the job done."

"Thanks, man. It will be great to see you guys. And, hey, don't forget to make those chicken wings." Praying hard struck up a major appetite.

"You got it. See you in a few days."

After I hung up the phone, I let out a big sigh. I think I may have even smiled a bit. I loved those guys. I knew they'd have my back. I left the bedroom and entered the TV room where my wife was watching some show on Netflix that I had no interest in.

"We're meeting this Thursday. Is that OK?"

I don't even know why I asked. Thursday night prayer meeting was the one place she let me—encouraged me—to go without hesitation.

By the time Thursday evening dinner rolled around, I was a whirling dervish of excitement. I couldn't wait to make the drive to see my dudes.

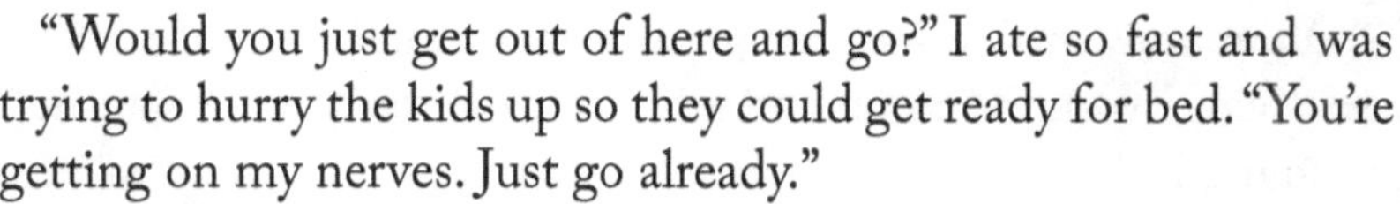

"Would you just get out of here and go?" I ate so fast and was trying to hurry the kids up so they could get ready for bed. "You're getting on my nerves. Just go already."

"Alright, babe. I'll see you later. I'll probably be pretty late."

"Tell Theresa I said hello."

"I probably won't see her. She usually stays out of the way when we come over."

"OK, but if you do see her, give her my love."

"I will." I bent down to her chair and gently kissed her cheek. "I'll see you later."

"Drive safe."

Admittedly, I did not want to drive for an hour, but I couldn't wait to see my boys. Time flew by as I traversed the highways and back country roads. I hadn't seen my guys in over a year. Camille and I had relocated when I started at the church.

When I pulled into Brent's driveway, I grinned as I saw familiar cars. *Tony's here. Brandon and Daniel too. It's going to be a good one.*

I didn't bother to knock. I just walked in the front door. *This is my brother's house. What do I need to knock for? I'm no guest.* The gang had gathered in the kitchen. "Hey y'all!"

Brandon was the first to greet. "Bobbay!" He gave me a bear hug. "I'm so glad you're here. It hasn't been the same since you left."

"Good to see you too, man." Noticing Theresa in the pantry, I turned to address her. "Hey, girl. Camille sends her love."

"Aww, I miss her. How's my girl doing?"

"Well, not the best, I have to admit. But that's mostly my fault as usual. That's why I'm here tonight. I need y'all's prayers."

"Please share my greetings with her." Theresa paused awkwardly, "Well, don't let me stop you. I'll get out of your way and let you boys do your thing." She picked up a bowl of popcorn and exited the room. I followed her with my eyes. As she passed the stove, I noticed the red numbers on the oven.

The wings are in there.

Brent spoke up, "Let's go downstairs, fellas."

He led the way down to his man cave. Two couches and a couple chairs shaped a semi-circle. "Bobby, what's going on, man?"

"Oh, man, Camille has her panties in a bunch because a few weeks ago I was preaching and admitted I struggle with internet pornography."

Brandon cackled aloud. "You did what?"

As was his way, Brent tried to rationalize, "In a sermon? What'd your pastor say?"

"Get this. He thanked me for my honesty. He said we need more transparency in the church. When I told Camille, that's when all hell broke loose."

"Wait. You told her *after* you told the congregation?" Laughing with incredulity he added, "Boy, you crazy!" Brandon seemed to be leaning towards Camille's side.

"I didn't mean to. I kept arguing with the Spirit. I got the impression that the Lord wanted me to. To be honest. I forgot I was married to the Kraken. The confession seemed to fit the overall message of the sermon."

Brent broke in again, "So we need to pray for Bobby and Camille for sure, but what about you, Brandon?"

Brandon remained oddly quiet. "Real talk?"

"That's right, Brandon. Real talk."

"Ain't nothing too bad. I got a massage at that little Asian place on the strip. It was going well, but before I knew it, Ling Ling had me finishing."

"What?" I screamed. "You got a happy ending?"

"It happened so fast. First, I was on my back and she was rubbing my thighs. She said something. I really didn't understand her. I was so relaxed I'm not sure I heard her right. Maybe she was asking for permission. I don't know. I said yes, and within seconds, *whoo!*"

"How are you laughing right now? You're confessing to cheating on your wife."

"I didn't cheat. It was the language barrier, dude."

"Bruh, you cheat every time you pull up Porn Hub or whatever site. Remember what Jesus said," Brandon asserted, *But I say unto you, That whosoever looketh on a woman to lust after her hath committed adultery with her already in his heart.* You cheated, Bro."

"I beg to differ. Looking at hot models or those you're attracted to and don't know them in person is very common. I don't consider that cheating. It's a little different than having a woman who is not your wife touch you in real life. Have you told your wife?"

"Heck no!"

"Why? Because you cheated! Did you even feel bad?"

"It was an accident, dude. Nothing to tell."

Ever the level-headed, observant one, Brent queried, "Tony, you've barely even said two words. What's going on with you?"

Tony grabbed the throw pillow on the couch next to him and squeezed it tightly into his stomach. "Guys, my life is falling apart. I'm so glad you called me, Brent. I needed to come tonight. I need to be honest with you all. I have been cheating on my wife." He whispered. Facing Brandon, "And it's not an accident. The first time, it was, I guess."

"Wait! How do you *accidentally* have sex with someone who is not your wife? Did you slip and fall into it?"

"I guess you're right. There's this young girl at work. She wears the shortest skirts. I mean, this girl is fine! We were in the break room, and I was chatting her up. She looked at me in a way that said, *You can get with this.* I mean, I'm a married man, but a man nonetheless. And I ain't dumb. I leaped into action. That was the first and only time I ever cheated on my wife."

"Well…" he continued, "she's the only other woman. Since then, she's been hinting that she was going to take our relationship public." Unlike Brandon, Tony's tears seemed authentic. "I…love… my wife." He swallowed a big ball of air. "But this young trick is starting to make noise around the office, and them nosy people are starting to put two and two together. If Angel finds out, I'll lose her and the kids. I can't lose my kids, guys." A glob of snot fell from his nose. For a second, Tony did not speak, but he made an inarticulate noise between a grunt and a sniff. "I don't want to live like this. Oh, Jesus, please forgive me and help me!

Brent stood up and walked over to the 80s-era boom box in the corner. He pressed play and a somber saxophone belted from the speakers. It was instrumental, but I recognized the tune to "Love

Lifted Me," I learned the hymn when I was a young kid. It was #141 in the red hymnal we sang from on Sunday mornings.

I was sinking deep in sin,
  far from the peaceful shore,
very deeply stained within,
  sinking to rise no more.
But the master of the sea
  heard my despairing cry,
and from the waters lifted me,
  now safe am I.

Brent turned and addressed the gathering. "Gentlemen, let's pray. We're praying for Bobby J and Camille, for Tony and Angel—that their marriages can sustain these present trials, and that these men can make it right with God and find forgiveness for their souls. Brandon, I don't know what to pray for you, but you do need prayer."

Brent cracked a quick smile in Brandon's direction. The music reached the chorus.

Love lifted me,
  love lifted me,
when nothing else could help,
  love lifted me.

I knelt beside the sofa and buried my face into the cushions. I bitterly wept as I implored God for help. The music set the tone for the work that would happen in the room that night.

At some point, I felt a strong hand on my back. My own begging ceased long enough for me to recognize Brent's deep baritone voice calling out my name in prayer—praying for strength and God's holy power and grace to stand against the enemy. I sighed as I felt peace overwhelm me. *He's got my back.*

I returned the favor when I laid my hand on Tony's shoulder. I called out, "Savior, please help my friend. He needs you. He recognizes his faults and the sin he's committed, and I plead with him for your sweet forgiveness flooding his life. Where he's weak, make him strong, and give him the anointing he needs to destroy the yoke of bondage from his mind. In Jesus' name."

I knelt beside him and took his right hand into my own. I bent my head left to connect with his. *I hoped he got my message.* Just then, he pushed back with his own head.

I stood up and returned to my original position. I sat and waited in silence as I watched the others complete their orations. I peered around the room and took note of the numerous changes Brent had made to the room since I was last here. The wallpaper had turned pink—so much for a man-cave. Theresa had some pull, I surmised. I reached for a tissue from the box on the end table. I brushed the trophy Brent kept on the table as a vestige of his athletic past many years and many pounds earlier. I snorted into the tissue and wiped the tears from my eyes. I tilted my head back and slid down to allow the music to wash over me in peace.

Lord, thank you for these men you've placed in my life. I now know it wasn't just chance that brought me to them. You clearly orchestrated it for my good, and I'm grateful. Thank you.

We walked upstairs together. Brent opened the oven and produced what looked like a vat of chicken appendages. Before we ate, he pulled a bag of lettuce from the refrigerator, busted open the bag, and pulled a handful of green Romaine bites. He turned up a bottle of ranch dressing above his gaping lips and guzzled a squirt.

Shrugging his shoulders, all he said was, "Atkins."

The fellas chuckled.

"You haven't changed one bit." I looked him in his eyes. "And, I hope you never do. Love you, boy."

As I left the house, Brent walked me back to my car. His classic parting words, "I re-joyed you."

12

I had much to think about on my hour drive from Brent's. I was feeling pretty high spiritually. I took an exit to head on the necessary route. Within moments, my eyes beheld "Adult Depot" in neon lights. I recognized this spot as one of the old haunts where I sat in one of those little booths. It was still a little way off in the distance. I steeled myself against the urge to turn in. *I will not turn into that lot. I will NOT turn into that lot. I WILL NOT TURN INTO THAT LOT!*

I kept driving, and as I began to pass, something took over the steering wheel. I Daytona-style careened left barely missing being smashed by the speeding eighteen-wheeler on the opposite side of the highway. The driver blasted his horn, and I skidded onto the gravel parking lot. Within seconds, I had slipped a dollar into the machine.

How did I get here again?

I returned to the car with much shame in my heart and much fewer dollars in my wallet.

Why do I always feel shame after *but never* before *I fail?*

Brent made sense earlier. Sometime during our repast, he leaned over to me and said, "My church has a support group for men who struggle with porn. Maybe you should check to see if there's something like that in your area? Or maybe seek out a therapist who could help you?"

I had sloughed his recommendation off, because I had always considered therapists were for the *sick*. Pulling back onto the highway from the parking lot, I said, "Maybe I am sick," into the darkness. I committed at that moment I would find a support group or a therapist—and *soon*.

The next morning, I checked the yellow pages for *men's support groups*. I found one listed at a Presbyterian church about ten minutes from my house. In my head, Presbyterian meant *white*. I was raised to believe white folks and black folks had different issues, and that black people should steer clear of white *help*. I had been attending a white church for a few years. Gethsemane was white because Pastor Craft was white. I had already taken enough community flack for joining the staff.

I'll never forget coming out of the local grocery story when I was relatively new to the area. Camille and I were approached by a black man who introduced himself as Bishop Something-or-Other. He invited us to join his church. When I told him we were going to Gethsemane, he declared we were going *to that white man's church* and condemned us to hell. I could only imagine my fate going to a white denomination's support group for help.

I called the listed number and found out the group met on Tuesday evenings at 6:00. I set the date in my calendar to attend the next meeting.

Nervous as heck as I walked down the sidewalk to the side door of the large brick edifice that had been painted white. It looked like the church had been there for centuries. The cemented cornerstone confirmed the church had existed since 1885.

I arrived a few minutes late, and the group had already started. Not wanting to interrupt, I slid into the first empty seat I saw. An older gentleman with grey wispy hair addressed the circle. I imagined he was the leader. He held a Styrofoam cup of what appeared to be black coffee. He sipped before he spoke.

"The more pornography a man watches, the more he needs to conjure images of pornography to maintain arousal and will be more likely to ask for particular sexual acts with his partner and have concerns over his sexual performance and body image."

I nodded in agreement. I have done that. Camille called me on it, too.

One night, we shared a romantic evening. I wanted to try

something new I had seen in a movie. It looked really good, and the woman seemed to be pleased. Unlike my expectation, Camille stopped mid-stream with alarmed dissent, "What are you doing? Where'd you learn that from?"

Discouraged, I made a mental note not to try that again.

Al, the grey-haired leader, noticed me in the back corner despite my trying to be invisible. "I'm seeing some newer faces here tonight. I'm Al, and I want to welcome you to Truth Finders. It is our goal to help men separate themselves from the lies they've believed about sex and sexuality the porn industry has taught them. This is a confidential support group, and what you say here will be kept in the strictest confidence. We make a covenant with each other to protect each other from sharing anything you hear from someone else in this space. This is a judgment-free zone, and we want to preserve people from being revealed. We are each on a private journey, but we want no one to feel like they're in this alone. You are not alone."

As if on cue, the men seated in the circle in unison collectively chorused, "You are not alone."

Al opened the floor to the brothers to share their personal victories and struggles of the past week. Charles was the first to share, but I didn't hear much beyond his name because Al handed me a questionnaire he wanted returned to him at the end of the night. He expected me to pull a pen from his breast pocket. I filled my name and a bunch of other info on the dotted line. I read the first few questions and got a little uneasy. *Did I really want to reveal all this stuff to a bunch of strangers?*

The questions got really deep really quickly. They wanted to know about sexual abuse, sexual orientation, about sexual behaviors that I may have been arrested for, whether I had *subscribed to or regularly purchased/rented sexually explicit magazines or videos.* Well, duh! I got both tickled by the questions related to my preoccupation with thoughts about sex, and whether these thoughts got in the way of my romantic relationships. My thoughts turned towards Camille when they asked, *Does your significant other(s), friends, or family ever worry or complain about your sexual behavior? (not related to sexual orientation)?*

The questions turned towards whether I was having trouble paying for phone expenses because of my sexual proclivities. I considered how many times I had created new online accounts to keep my phone sex calls hidden. People calling me at work must have been frustrated by the busy signal on my office phone. Kids today would never appreciate the benefit of broadband Wi-Fi internet service.

The next questions brought me back to Camille. "Has your involvement with pornography, phone sex, computer board sex, etc. become greater than your intimate contacts with romantic partners?" I can't recall the numbers of times I complained of being *too tired* when I resisted her advances as I thought I would not be able to measure up.

Boy, they are thorough!

When the questions asked about frequenting video bookstores as a regular part of sexual activities, I transported back to my college days sneaking in the back room of the video store to secretly rent a VCR tape to watch when my roommate was out. I felt so dirty emerging from behind the curtain. *What if someone from the gospel choir or the Bible study group was out there?* Still not enough to make me quit.

I thought about the poor victims of pedophiles when the survey questioned if I had ever had sex with a minor. *Disgusting! I'm not that sick!* I believe there is a special compartment in hell for those who sexually abuse children. *There's too many people giving it away for free; no one should have to force a child. It's rape, people.*

Some of the questions I struggled to answer truthfully. Not because I was trying to lie, but the questions invited duplicity. For instance, the only response is yes or no, but the question, "Are you HIV positive, yet continue to engage in risky or unsafe sexual behavior?" is really two questions. I could honestly answer that I am not HIV positive, but weren't they asking if I also engaged in risky sexual behavior?

Michael was next. He shifted nervously. I could tell he was anxious; he adjusted his hoodie often. From the way he began, I could tell he was not new to the self-revelation process.

"I saw hardcore pornography for the first time around the first or second grade. The effects it had on my life were similar to those of abuse. I was reintroduced to porn at a bookstore as a middle-schooler. Those were hard years for me, and porn felt like a relief—something good in the midst of something bad. I was hooked."

He paused before continuing. "I came to Christ at a young age and grew up in church, but there was always a dark side to me. I began feeling guilty in high school but learned it was better not to talk about it. I thought I needed to figure it out on my own, just Jesus and me." He turned towards the group. He wanted to make sure we could hear him. He stroked his beard. "Maybe you're fighting a similar battle. Maybe you're fighting one now or know someone who is. You're not alone."

On cue again, the men repeated the group's mantra.

Michael continued. "When I was 21, I attended Bible school and later entered full-time Christian ministry. I brought my pornography addiction with me. I lived two lives, and my shame started to grow. I didn't understand why I was powerless over this sexual darkness, so I hid that life at whatever cost."

A guy wearing plaid pants stood up and walked over to the refreshments table. He returned with coffee and a glazed donut.

"I took a year away from ministry to focus on restoration. It was a great year, but it didn't help with my addiction. I attended counseling, but that didn't help with my addiction either. I believed Jesus wanted to transform me, but I could not understand why he wouldn't heal this area. I decided either I was broken beyond repair ,or that, maybe, God wasn't real. I was in despair, completely hopeless. I had tried everything and eventually stopped believing I could be free."

I know that feeling.

Michael continued. "A chance encounter with Charles Harper, founder of Pure Desire Ministries, resulted in me and my wife beginning his counseling and recovery program. I had finally met a Christian man who could make sense of what was happening in my life. Charles and his wife navigated us through sexual addiction counseling integrated with a biblical worldview.

"I learned that at the core of sexual bondage, there's often an intimacy wound. Now when I struggle, I understand why and have resources to help. My intimacy wounds are healing, and I'm learning how to trust my wife and the Lord with all of me. I can now say I've had three years of solid sobriety with no acting out. I'm taking what I learned from Ted and teaching others because this topic is something people are desperate to hear."

Three years. It's gonna take that long?

Michael was the last to share. Al broke in and called for a conclusion. He played a song for everyone. "I think these words will minister to you all here." He pressed play on his CD player. The melody started. I was surprised by the soulful tunes coming through the speaker. I would never have expected this at a Presbyterian church. Soon a male soloist began crooning about how God loved him through the good and the bad. The part that touched me deeply happened when the singer added that God didn't erase his future because of you past mistakes.

A tear escaped my left eye. I wiped it away quickly for fear of appearing weak in front of all these men.

Al found his way over to me after he had shook a few hands. I assumed he wanted the questionnaire back, so I extended it to him in advance.

He took it from my hand and looked at it. "Bobby, it was great to have you here tonight. I hope you'll come back."

"Yes, I believe I will." I smiled and reassured him I enjoyed myself. "I didn't know what to expect, but the meeting exceeded my expectations, especially that last song."

"Well, let me hype you to another song that has ministered to me the Rev. Daryl Coley. The lyrics declare that God has already forgotten those thing we can't seem to forget and still regret. God answers an honest prayer with mercy."

Man, this guy gets it!

Al kept ministering to me. "I serve a god of forgiveness. People forget that. He throws our sins into the sea of forgetfulness. As far as the east is from the west, he remembers our sins no more."

"Thank you, Al. I needed that reminder."

Reaching to shake my hand, he replied, "Hey, we all do."

✝✝✝

One night at Truth, Al produced a sermonic video by Ted Haggard. I listened as he preached "Living as if there are No Secrets." By this time he had been defrocked as leader of the National Evangelical Association, and it seemed fraudulent and disingenuous to hear him preach "Sin will take your farther than you want to go; it will cost you more than you want to pay. It will keep you longer than you want to stay." The date on the video stamped nearly two years before his own struggle with sexual impropriety with a male prostitute and alleged drug abuse had been revealed. His oddly prophetic commentary exposed the spiritual tug-of-war operating in me.

Intrigued by Haggard's words, I wanted to do some digging around for more info on his case. This case was a national scandal. There were all kinds of social media comments calling him a hypocrite and a Sodomite, but I was more interested in hearing *his* side of the story. His church had posted some interesting words on their website. The overseers of the church posted a letter indicating that Pastor Haggard had *demonstrated immoral conduct* and that they felt it necessary *to remove the pastor from his position or to discipline him in any way they deem necessary.*

They also had posted a letter from Haggard's wife, Gayle, that struck me as eerily similar. In the letter she said she was standing by her husband *till death,* and she suggested that this problem is evidence that they did not live a perfect existence; she could relate to the problems of the people.

I turned my eyes from the computer screen and stared at my wife's picture in the gilded frame setting atop my desk and I wondered at how lucky I was to have such a dedicated partner. I needed to do right by her. I needed to get real honest with myself about getting better.

About a month later, I was in the laundry room when my older son walked in. I had to tell him. He didn't know that I knew about his own struggles in that same arena. I couldn't scold him—or so I thought——for doing the same thing that I was doing; so rather than being a conscientious parent, I had let him wallow in the muck

too. I couldn't hold out anymore though; both of our freedoms were in the mix.

"Son, we need to talk." I paused as he got the look on his face—that one that screamed, *I don't know what I got caught doing, but I hope it's not too bad.*

"Yeah, Dad, what's up?"

I told him that I knew about his problem, and that he needed to stop using the family computer for viewing pornography, not only because it was wrong but because his younger siblings had access to that same computer.

"In all honesty, though," I admitted, "I have a problem. I've checked the history on that computer, and you've been downloading some strange stuff. Do you need to talk to me about anything?"

"Dad, you wouldn't understand." His sheepish look made me believe that either he was really embarrassed to talk to his dad about this stuff, or he really did think that I wouldn't understand.

Trying to sound all *Dad official*, I replied, "I want you to know that you can talk to me about anything. I love you, and there's nothing you can say or do that could make me love you any less."

He teared up a little. "Oh, Dad, I'm so ashamed. I'm a horrible person."

It's so hard to watch your boy go through feelings like this. I wanted to take his pain away.

"You're not a horrible person. I know exactly how you feel. You weren't in the service a couple weeks ago when I preached, but I testified that I, too, struggled with pornography. I have been trying to get this monkey off my back since I was your age."

"You do? But, you're a preacher. You shouldn't be looking at porn."

Chuckling, I added, "And you're a teenager. You shouldn't either."

"Dad, don't be a hypocrite!"

"I'm trying not to be—which is why I am talking to you about this. I need your help to stay clean. If I turn on this computer, I can't afford to be assaulted by pop-ups from my son's exploits online." I tried to be as stern as I could while maintaining my humility. "I have a problem. This is hard for me. Admitting this is hard. While I have you here, can you forgive me for my moral failing?"

"I'm not your judge, Dad. I have no right to forgive or not forgive you. You can do this. I believe in you."

"Maybe we can help each other? Do you want to stop?"

"I'm gonna be honest with you—I like it. It's not hurting anybody, so why stop?"

"You may think it doesn't hurt anybody. I could bore you with all the statistics and research about porn's impact upon relationships, how it teaches men and boys to mistreat women and how it creates unhealthy expectations about sex. But, I'm most concerned about your purity."

Frustrated, "Dad, don't worry. I'm still a virgin—unfortunately."

I could breathe again. That was a scary conversation. Not just hearing his desires to see his porn dreams realized, but that I was feeling disingenuous being a dad. I couldn't very well act like a spiritual leader on this issue while admitting that I suffered from the same problem, but it was necessary because I was trying to stay clean and could not afford to have the chance of seeing his files. His face was one of shock—I think for both of us.

James 5:16 instructs us to confess our faults to each other and pray for one another, that we may be healed. I never did find any more files of his on the computer; I certainly hope that my disclosure helped. Paul wrote in 1 Corinthians:

...to the weak I became as weak that I might gain the weak.

Maybe sharing the scars of secret sin with him saved him from the same pain.

And maybe it's time to get some professional help.

13

My fascination with porn was interrupting my life, and I was determined to get some help—professional help. The answer to my prayers arrived the very next day while pulling a shift at the post office.

I was taking a coffee break when I overheard my coworker Paula having a conversation with one of the mail carriers about the counseling program at her church and how great it was that the service was free because she couldn't afford it. After the mail carrier left, I apologized to Paula for appearing to eavesdrop and asked about the program.

"I thought I overheard you mention the service is free?" I stammered.

"Yes," Paula replied. "It is a ministry to the community."

"For real? Free? I know this guy who could sure use some counseling, but he can't afford much right now, and I... I mean, he... doesn't have insurance."

"No, seriously. Absolutely free."

"And it's open to the public? You don't have to be a member of your church?"

"Nope, completely free and open to the public. Just have your friend give 'em a call."

I raised my eyebrows a titch. In my experience, most churches only provide services for their own people. This had to be ordained by God.

"I'll have him call as soon as I get home. What's the name of your church again?"

"Restoration Ministries on Columbia Pike."

"Okay, thanks for the tip."

I spoke with the counselor, Liz, who was able to fit me in the following Thursday at 10:00. When I arrived at the church, the front doors were locked. Liz had given me instructions for my arrival, but I don't recall what she said. I tried peering through the glass doors. Thankfully, two older gentlemen were vacuuming in the lobby and saw me peeping. One of them came to door. "Can I help you, young man?"

"Yes, I'm here to see Liz in the Counseling Center."

"Oh, Liz. Let me show you the way." He invited me in.

"Would you like some coffee?" He pointed to a hospitality area where small Mr. Coffee pots beckoned.

"I think I will. I haven't had my cup yet." I filled my cup a little too full and coffee spilled onto the top of the white table. I reached for a napkin from the nearby stack. I made some stupid crack about how much I needed a cup o' joe. I took a sip and followed the old guy to Liz's office which was down a long corridor—last door on the left. It was basically a hole in the wall, converted storage closet. My usher knocked on the door and told Liz she had a visitor. Liz greeted me and extended her right hand. I shook it. The shake seemed weird. Her hands were cold and clammy. I talked myself out of making some off-hand comment about her fingers. It appeared to be a birth defect rather than accident, so I left it alone.

Liz welcomed me into her space and told me to sit down on the striped chair in front of her desk. I expected an older therapist, but Liz was a middle-aged lady with dark brown hair. Her costume jewelry screamed Dollar Store. She excused my tour guide and rounded her desk to sit behind it.

She handed me a two-page intake sheet for me to fill out by our next meeting. "Bobby, what brings you here today?

"Well, I have a problem." My somber tone set the mood for our discussion. "I'm a youth pastor at…" I started to name the church but reconsidered. "At a local church in the area."

She must have sensed my reticence to out myself and spoke up. "Bobby, it's important you know that everything you say here is private and confidential. It's just between us. Legally, I cannot speak about anything you disclose without your express permission. So, tell me what's going on. You say you have a problem?"

Feeling protected by the promise of anonymity, I opened my mouth and words fell out. "As I said, I am a youth pastor, and lately I've found myself attracted to a couple of ladies, who aren't my wife, at my church. If I'm perfectly honest, I've had some very bad thoughts about a them."

Liz leaned forward. "Now, I told you that I can't legally say anything you say to me, but I didn't tell you the whole thing. If you tell me anything that involves abuse of children and intent to harm yourself or others, I am obligated to report it to the authorities. Understand?"

"Yes, I do. And I, too, am a mandated reporter. And when I tell you the whole story, you'll understand the pickle I am in." I lowered my head and began speaking towards the ground. "I have been getting some help from the Truth Program at the Presbyterian church downtown. I have battled a pornography addiction for quite some time. Lately, I've been imagining some of the saints in my congregation in some not-so-holy ways."

"Is the program helping?"

"I thought it was, but I guess not enough. In fact, it's getting worse. It's not just porn anymore. It's creeping into my fantasies. I mean, some of the daydreams are vivid, and I worry about them becoming reality. I really want to stop, and my wife has really been hurt by all this."

"So, your wife knows? That's good that it's not a secret."

"But she doesn't know all this other stuff. I'm afraid I might do something I'll regret. My job requires I be in close proximity to the women sometimes. What's more is we get into some intimate discussions. They often confide in me about their problems with men and with their lives. My wife watches *Lifetime* movies and true crime documentaries, and I know how easily I could be *grooming* these women. I try to put up guards and protections just to be safe. My senior pastor cautions the team to not be alone with a person of the opposite sex, but it's virtually impossible." I paused the conversation. "Uhh, do you mind if I use the restroom?"

"No, go right ahead. It's down the hall. When you can, turn right and the bathroom sits right on the corner."

I excused myself and followed her directions. When I got back, Liz tapped a stack of papers on her desk. I returned to my seat, and she started asking questions, encouraging me to open up about my life. She was good at it too. Before I knew it, she said, "Bobby, it's been nearly an hour, and I believe our time is just about up for today. We'll pick this up next time *if* you wish to continue meeting."

"Yes I do. How much do I owe you for today?"

"Nothing. It's free."

"Well, that's good to know. Are you sure?"

"It's a service of the church made possible by generous donations."

"Oh, that's good."

"How about we set something up for this same time next week?"

I smiled. "That sounds like a good plan. This time is usually free for me. I'll see you next week." Not wanting to shake her cold hands again, I did not extend my hand when we said our goodbyes.

When I got to the car, I made a mental note to be sure to fill out the intake form before our next meeting, then I folded the form and slid it into the sun visor.

I got back to my house around 11:30 a.m. I started prepping to cook dinner for Camille to show her how much I appreciated her. She likes when I grill, so I decided to make Blackberry Balsamic BBQ Sauce fresh from scratch. It's an easy recipe. I had stopped at the local grocery store to pick up some essentials. It made me happy to walk in the front door and find blackberries were on sale buy-one-get-one-free. I really love end of summer sales on fresh produce. I made sure to buy a couple extra pints so my son could have some. He always steals berries before I can cook them. This way, he could have his own container.

I put the berries in the blender with some balsamic vinegar , sugar, and some chicken broth. I whizzed that up and poured it into a saucepan and set that on the heat the reduce and thicken. As it got to the right consistency, I got my charcoal ready. By the time Camille walked in the house, the aroma intoxicated the house. I also prepared some roasted asparagus.

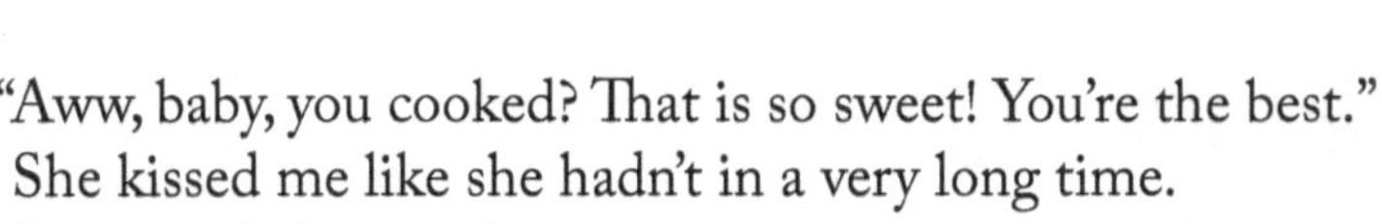

"Aww, baby, you cooked? That is so sweet! You're the best."

She kissed me like she hadn't in a very long time.

I may get lucky tonight.

"I even made dessert. It's a pumpkin dump cake—a *pump* cake as your daughter called it. Eat hearty. The coffee's fresh and the dessert warm. A nice scoop of vanilla ice cream will set that off! And, don't worry about the dishes. I'll get those too. Just set yourself in *my* chair and relax. I've got you tonight."

"What did I do to deserve all this?"

"Just wanted to do something nice for you. I love you, girl."

"What did *you* do then? I don't trust all this love all of a sudden."

Man, I messed this chick up. How can she stand there with her hands on her hips angrily doubting me? I've only been cooking for five hours to get this meal ready for her.

14

"**I**t's been a long time since I've been here. I've missed you guys."

Several months had gone by since I made it to Truth. As soon as Al opened the floor, I jumped at the chance to talk.

"I'll go."

I bounced in my chair with my hand raised like I was bidding on an auction.

"I have to tell the truth, though; I thought I didn't need you guys anymore. I felt I had a handle on things. Our church picnic happened a week or so ago. We went to Fun World Amusement Park for the day. I really thought I was healed. I was in line for their big new roller coaster. There was this cute young lady right in front of me. She had golden-brown skin, and I was immediately attracted. She seemed to be maybe seventeen or eighteen. She wore a bikini top that fit her snugly in all the right ways. Her striped bikini bottoms were on display too. I saw them because she had unzipped her denim cutoffs and opened the button. The teen boys who had been in front of her obviously noticed too, because they never really took their eyes off of her. They ogled, pointed, and whispered to each other. It was clear that were turned on by the sight. Having been *like* them, I knew exactly what they were considering as they muttered and chuckled. Ordinarily, I'd be interested in her myself. *Ordinarily*," I emphasized, "this sight would have triggered something in *me*."

I interrupted myself, "Wait. It did trigger something in me. Profound sadness and pity. I imagined this young lady was my daughter, and I felt an obligation not to see her as an object of sexual gratification, but as someone who didn't know any better." I explained how I had kept my eyes on her and the boys as the line slowly progressed between rides.

"As it so happened, the girl was a lone rider. The college kid running the ride called aloud for a single rider to fill the space next to her. I took that as a sign I was meant to say something to her—to minister to her in some way."

I realized I was talking way too fast. I took a deep breath and consciously slowed the pace of my speech. "As the operator did the final safety checks and tightened our seat belts, I took the time to introduce myself to her saying, 'Hi, I'm Bobby."

She greeted me back and I noticed the young men had somehow gotten behind us and were still corralled in line.

"You see those guys over there? They've been checking you out. You're a pretty girl, and they've been talking about you and looking inappropriately at you. I've been young once, so I can imagine what they've been thinking. You may want to considering covering yourself up a bit. I mean, all of your *business* is out in the street."

"Who, them?" She pointed in their general direction."

"Yes, them. Those three right there. One of them made an inappropriate gesture about the size of your chest. If you were my daughter, I would hope somebody would say something to you." She said 'OK' and began to straighten up her clothing.

"I felt I had done the right thing. We finished the ride, and we exchanged pleasantries." Smiling, I continued my story, "I ran into her again a few hours later after I had reconnected with my family. We exchanged *knowing* glances. I did notice her clothes were fixed properly. I knew I had made an impact for the kingdom."

I breathed a sigh of relief before I concluded my spiel with a thought, "I felt like I had turned a corner. Like I possessed a new superpower. Suddenly, I no longer alone. I felt all of your strength behind me cheering me on."

I explained how that brief moment of victory had sustained me over this past time—until this morning when I tripped and fell.

Al broke in. "Bobby, this is one of the tricks of the enemy. In his first letter to the Corinthians, the Apostle Paul cautioned, *If you think you are standing strong, be careful, for you, too, may fall into the same sin.*" He looked out towards the other men in the circle saying, "Part of your continued freedom will depend upon knowing and understanding your triggers. These are your vulnerability points. A trigger is anything that makes you vulnerable to your former lusts or behaviors: perhaps sudden stress, pain, or discomfort, or a glimpse at a magazine. For example, I sometimes have to avoid looking at women's clothing and undergarment catalogs."

Al seemed so strong in his personal commitments, I had not imagined that he struggled also.

"Some of us must also acknowledge how our personal relationships may need to change. Sometimes, even hanging around with certain people makes us vulnerable."

We would not escape his wisdom tonight. "You need to understand that once a triggering event happens, we can have some level of internal dysfunction. These symptoms can include difficulty in thinking clearly, managing feelings and emotions, and moments of remembrance where we mistakenly see our former behaviors as positive; the recovery specialists refer to this as euphoric recall—we remember the *good* but ignore the immensity of the negative."

Al got onto his soapbox. He sat forward, and I imagined a Pentecostal preacher was trying to break out of him.

"On his last night of earthly ministry, Jesus and his disciples had retired to the Garden of Gethsemane to pray. Before breaking off from the group for a few moments of solitude, Jesus spoke to his disciples and said, *Watch* and *pray, that ye enter not into temptation.* What I'm suggesting is, Jesus was teaching them *and* us that being aware of the possibility of temptation is the effective method of staying out of trouble. He knew it is easier *never to* than break the habit.

"I've said this before, and I'll never stop saying it—temptation itself is not sin; in essence, a temptation is just a thought that pops into our heads; most often as a result of carnal living. It is when we consider that thought as a viable option that it becomes sin. So the battle starts there in your mind. Do you have your battle gear on? The last vestments of the whole armor of God as defined in Ephesians 6:17 are *the helmet of salvation and the sword of the Spirit, which is the word of God.* I find it interesting that salvation is what guards the mind—when tempting thoughts arise, start fighting with this declaration: *I'm saved!* This statement reflects the resurrecting power of Jesus Christ; in that declarative statement I acknowledge that according to Romans 6:2 I am dead to sin. When you learn to stop tempting thoughts right at the outset, you will find greater success in the battle."

Several men, including myself, acknowledged the rightness of Al's words with resounding *Amens* and *That's the truths*.

"I'm going to close the floor to further stories right now, because I feel an urge to share more from The Word tonight.

"As you know, there is typically a pattern to our thoughts triggered by temptations. So let's interrupt our thought processes towards evil deeds and develop a new strategy for victory. Philippians 4:8 defines a proactive rather than reactive approach to the thoughts that enter our mind. Paul writes that we ought to fill our minds and meditate on *whatsoever things are true, whatsoever things are honest, whatsoever things are just, whatsoever things are pure, whatsoever things are lovely, whatsoever things are of good report.*

"Regularly thinking about these things can be preemptive as they rid our thoughts of wickedness; they also provide an excellent manner of judging the worth or appropriateness of any particular activity. Go ahead—pause right here and think about your temptations—do they pass muster in light of this passage? When you are tempted, quickly scrutinize whether the thought, if it became action, would be pure, right, truthful, honest, etc. Would you be able to give a good report? Think about standing in front of your congregation and testifying if you did the action? Does it line up with God's Word, his will for your life, and your purpose as a witness for Christ?"

I thought, *Now, that's a good point.*

Al continued, "Once you become skilled at testing the merit of a tempting thought, you must be willing to take *the hard right instead of the easy left* and not give in to the desire. Making this decision shows your willingness to follow Christ; it also shows that you are actively engaged in your own emancipation. King Solomon, the wisest man in the world advised: *A prudent person sees trouble coming and ducks; a simpleton walks in blindly and is clobbered.* God promises the escape route, but you have to take the turn to avoid trouble."

He brought it home now. "When all else fails—*run!* Did you know that the Bible gives you an out in the face of the pressure of temptation? Check this out. He says to flee fornication. Flee from idolatry. Flee these things. Flee also youthful lusts.

"Quit trying to act like Superman! You are not less than a man if you say you can't handle the situation. God would rather you be wholly holy than worry about some mythic notions about masculinity. Even superheroes have their weaknesses. Ever heard of Kryptonite?"

Al was serious. He emphasized the crucial role of holiness for men. I recalled a recent breakfast meeting I'd had with Pastor Craft and the conversation turned this exact subject. I had asked Pastor to just get real with me.

"Make it practical," I said. "What does it mean to *flee youthful lusts?*" I asked, seated across the breakfast table. My BLT with eggs was not so important at that moment.

Craft answered, "You need to remove yourself from the situation. If it's television, you just need to go to a different place. If it's on your computer, get away from it. Change rooms. Get away from that thing." He paused a few seconds to cut the pancakes he had previously slathered with butter. He took a big bite, chewed a few times, and barely swallowed. His mouth still kinda full, he continued, "In the face of temptations, consider the following assessment from Colossians 3:17 *And whatsoever ye do in word or deed, do all in the name of the Lord Jesus, giving thanks to God and the Father by him.*"

He washed the pancakes down with a swill from his teacup. "The Bible teaches that following the leading of the Spirit is crucial for righteousness, holiness, avoiding failure, and being one who overcomes. I want to give you the following guidelines as a method for living a principled walk with the Lord. And since the Bible does not always specifically speak out against a variety of 21st century possibilities for sin, this list of questions can help determine the

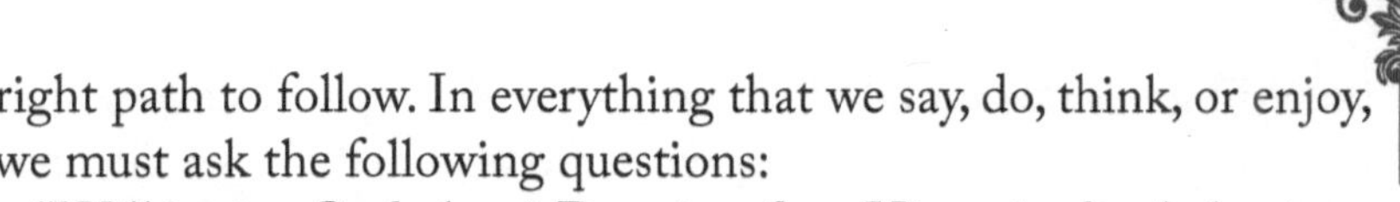

right path to follow. In everything that we say, do, think, or enjoy, we must ask the following questions:

"Will it give God glory? Does it reflect His attitudes, behaviors, or power?

"If Jesus were standing next to you, would you do it? Would you do the action *in the name of Jesus?*

"Would you ask God's blessing upon the activity? Would you offer him thanks for it?

"Would Jesus himself have done the activity while living on earth?

"If another Christian saw me doing this, how would I feel? How would that Christian respond to seeing me?

"Will it weaken my desire for spiritual things, God's Word, and prayer?

"If an unsaved person saw me doing the act, how would I respond? How effective would I be able to witness to that unsaved person? Could I introduce Christ to that person while doing the activity?"

Pastor Craft explained how so much of arresting temptations before we become agents of sin is determined long before the moment of temptation. "You must have a made-up mind that you are alive in Christ and dead to a life of sin. The Book of Job declares, *I made a covenant with my eyes not to look with lust upon a young woman.*"

✝✝✝

Accountability and discipline must have been the thing to address, because Pastor Craft and Al both addressed it.

In our previous meeting, Al sat straight up in his chair. "Now, say what you will about the efficacy of 12-step programs, but one of the concepts they teach can be very effective in avoiding, escaping, and overcoming temptation—unconditional abstinence, no matter what. When you are freed from the bondage of sin, you need to steer clear of anything that looks, sounds, or smells like the former temptation. What happens so often, unfortunately, is that we intentionally go looking for the *close-enough* line. For instance, after a season of success, a person who was freed from a pornography addiction will not go to the XXX section of the video store, but will get a racy rated-R movie that is simply soft core rather than hardcore. The person gets the same thrill with less guilt, and a little bit of self-righteousness, because after all, *I didn't get the porn*. We must not go looking for reasons, ways, and excuses to relapse into old behaviors. Complacency and self-confidence are your enemies; don't get too comfortable and forget that the enemy does not want to see you free.

"Many people who know me know that I am a big movie buff, and one of my favorites is *The Wiz*. You have probably seen *The Wizard of Oz*, the movie that made Judy Garland a household name. Well, *The Wiz* is what I will call the *colorized* version. Filmed in the late 1970s, this movie has quite a star-studded lineup, including Diana Ross as Dorothy, Nipsy Russell as the Tin Man, Richard Pryor as the Wiz, Lena Horne playing Glinda the Good Witch, and a normal Michael Jackson as the Scarecrow.

"The stories don't vary much from each other," Al explained. "Dorothy is transported into a magical land; kills a witch; the witch's sister gets mad and tries to kill Dorothy; Dorothy meets some friends who are each looking for some external validation. They dance and sing their way to the Emerald City to speak to the great and powerful Wizard of Oz.

"Soon after arriving in Oz, Dorothy learns that she has accidentally killed the Wicked Witch of the East and is rewarded the ruby slippers worn by the decedent. Dorothy is instructed to never remove the slippers until she returns to her native country —Kansas, in *The Wizard of Oz*, but Harlem, New York, in *The Wiz*. Evillene, the Wicked Witch of the West, goes to great lengths to coerce Dorothy into giving her the ruby slippers, which apparently held great power. She tortures Dorothy's companions and even threatens to throw little Toto into a fiery furnace. Seeing her friends in peril, Dorothy is confused—should she ignore the instructions to save her friends? Just then, the Cowardly Lion yells out, *Don't give up the shoes, Dorothy!*

"*Don't give up the shoes!* What a profound statement from such a cowardly creature," Al mused. "It reveals an important lesson for us—our salvation is a treasure and should be guarded with every ounce of our beings. In essence, the Lion's admonishment was to hold on to the very thing that gives us overcoming power."

"You see, even Evillene, with all her magic, was powerless against those shoes. When she tried to use her powers to take the shoes, her fingers folded backwards and crippled her hand. Dorothy was untouchable as long as she was wearing those ruby slippers. Those shoes would become the symbol of Dorothy's authority.

"Similarly, the body of Christ must learn to operate within the realm of kingdom authority that we have been given. In the Genesis account, when God created Adam, he gave Adam one thing: dominion. When Adam sinned, his punishment was a loss of God's life within him resulting in both moral and spiritual death. Their former relationship to God was destroyed, and consequently, Satan gained dominion, becoming the *prince of this world*. The grace of God is such that when Christ died he took dominion and gave it back to us. You are not powerless for you are not alone."

The league chanted, "You are not alone," as Al took up the mantle again.

"We must recognize that the battle being waged for our souls is about one thing: dominion—who is going to have control of your life and future. Through Christ, *you* have it. Satan wants it back, but don't give in.

"Well, look at the time." Al looked at his watch. "Let me end here with this thought. Near the end of *The Wiz,* Dorothy was considering giving up because it appeared all hope was lost. All of her friends were facing death and destruction, and she could not see a way out. The Lion's words stopped her on her path towards conceding. Let me remind you that in this version of the story, the witch was running a sweatshop in a dilapidated warehouse. Moments later, as one of the witch's henchmen was carrying Toto towards the furnace, Dorothy pulled the fire alarm and turned the sprinklers on. The witch screamed and declared that she was allergic to water and began to melt into her throne, which coincidentally, was actually a giant bronze toilet. After Evillene's demise, the sprinkling water began to wash away the filth from the windows and the sunlight began to shine through. A breeze began to blow away the dust and dirt from the floor.

"Soon, the imprisoned, hideously deformed sweatshop workers began to be transformed; their prison was not jails or bars, but grotesque costumes that covered them from head to toe. As the waters ran and the sun shone, what had once been dark and ugly, what had been binding them began to fall off. The workers emerged from the cocoons of bondage and glistened in their new golden outfits that reflected the sunlight. When they realized that their enemy was no longer a threat to them, they cheered and broke into song and dance—*The Wiz* is a musical after all. Their song of choice was titled "Can't You Feel a Brand New Day?" The scene was reminiscent of a good old-fashioned Pentecostal praise service! It's not the normal way we end these meetings, but can't you feel a brand-new day?"

15

The his day, Liz changed our regularly scheduled appointment time because her church leadership had called a staff meeting. At the appointed hour, I pulled up to the church to find a sign on the door indicating the counseling center had moved to a new location. The sign directed me to another entrance. I peeked in. Liz's new office was gorgeous. No longer a hole in the wall, it was much more spacious and welcoming.

"Hey, Bobby! C'mon in."

She greeted me like we were old college chums having a reunion. We talked briefly about family stuff and plans for the weekend. After fifteen minutes or so of chewing the fat, Liz got down to business. "Bobby, we've been seeing each other for nearly a year now, so I want to do an update to your treatment plan. When you first started to meet with me, you felt your life was spinning out of control because of a pretty serious pornography addiction. How have things been?"

"Much better, I think. Not perfect, but better. Less frequent. I feel more in control than I used to."

"If you don't mind me asking, why do you think you watch porn? What do you get from it?" She was not pulling any punches today.

"I wish I knew."

Not to be satisfied with these types of answers, Liz pushed on. I conceded. "I guess, I get motivated to please my wife more. I have never heard her moan like they do in the movies. The ladies always seem so satisfied."

"Bobby, you know those are often simulated sounds, right? They're actresses. None of it is real or natural."

"I know, but just once, I'd like to hear Camille make one of those sounds. I feel less than a man—like I'm not doing my job." Dejected, I tried to put up a machismo front. "I know it's all fake, Liz, but in the moment, it is real to me. I really want to satisfy her."

"Does anything you've watched seem to be helping?"

"Not really, no."

We talked more about what porn was doing for me for nearly an hour. I realized that my sense of self had improved. I admitted to feeling more victorious—not perfect, but stronger.

I shared with her how I had been thinking about some type of grand gesture to prove to Camille I was grateful for her forgiveness. She thought it a good idea, so I called Brent on my way home.

"Brent, I wanna do something crazy, and I need your help."

"Anything for you, Bro. What's on your mind? Lay it on me."

I poured out my idea to have a wives' day where we would make lunch for our wives and even wash their feet. Of course, we would pray for them.

"That's a killer idea! When do you want to do this?"

I pulled out my calendar and found a date when Camille would be off work. We compared potential dates and settled on a special date the following month.

16

Camille was not one for surprises. The drive to Brent's was long and she peppered with questions about what we were doing.

"Just relax," I told her, "You're in good hands."

When we pulled up to Brent's house, the other ladies were all sitting on the front porch.

"Why are y'all out here?" Camille asked quizzically.

"We're not allowed inside. The men need the space to get ready. Thank God it's relatively warm today." Theresa, Brent's wife, intoned.

"It's so good to see everybody! It's been too long," Camille said.

"Too long, indeed. I'm so glad my girls are all here." Angela's flat tone belied her excitement.

"How have you all been? How are the kids?" Camille wondered as she swung on the child's swing set in the front yard.

"A mess just like they daddy!" All the ladies chuckled at Theresa's slight insult.

"Well, I'm going in. I'll see y'all later." I snickered as I entered the house leaving the rest of the ladies to stew.

In just a little while, Tony ushered the women into the dining room where we served a filling lunch—all prepared by the husbands.

As host, Brent said the opening prayer. "Dear Father, thank you for what you have provided. Thank you for these women you have gifted us with. It is our plan to make you proud of us, as we do not take your gifts for granted. Now bless our food and our fellowship. Strengthen our bodies for the use in your service. In the name of Jesus, Amen."

"Ladies, this meal is in your honor. Eat hearty. I don't want to hear anything about diets. There are no calories in the food. I've already checked." He raised his glass in salute. "To my brothers, I salute you and the men you're becoming. Enjoy!" Brent took his seat at the head of the table amid the clinking of water glasses.

Angela was outdone. "Wait, y'all made this?"

"Yup. That's right. It's delicious and guilt-free."

Brent secreted himself into the kitchen and returned with a serving tray packed with his grilled barbecue ribs and chicken. "And ladies," he announced, "You'll want to leave room for Bobby's deep dish apple cobbler with candied pecans."

"Oh my! That sounds awesome! Have you never heard the saying, *Life is short. Eat dessert first?*" The ladies chuckled in agreement.

I really enjoyed the wives eating to their content. Each slurp and chew made it all worthwhile. It was nice to be all together again. Nothing had changed but the distance—it was just a group of family having Sunday meal together.

When it looked like the last chicken had been taken, I went into the kitchen and grabbed the apple pie. "Who wants dessert?"

Theresa emphatically cleared space. "Oh, I do."

Camille asked, "Is there coffee?"

Her request charged Brent in action. "Of course. I'll get it." He returned with a tray of mugs and cups and a carafe of coffee. The odd clinking of spoons on the tray clumsily rang out as he set the tray down on the table. "Who wants coffee?" He poured for whomever asked.

After lunch, Brent invited all the ladies to relax in the parlor. The men took their time hanging out in the kitchen while the ladies got comfy. They secretly needed a few moments to prepare for the next part of the plan.

"Brent, how is this going to work?" Tony asked to clarify the instructions for carrying out the foot washing.

"Each husband will bow before his wife and wash her feet. He'll make his prayers and pledges. In the interest of time, we'll do this all together at the same time. I know Bobby has to get back up the way to get his kids off the bus. We don't want to rush it, but this is important, so we want to take it seriously. I'll get us started, and then you guys come in." He prepared enough wash basins filled with warm water and soap for each of the women. He then gave each man a towel. He instructed them to follow him into the parlor.

Brent narrated as each husband filed in and knelt in front of his own wife. "Ladies, as Jesus was preparing for the Cross, He also prepped his Disciples by washing their feet. Today, we husbands are going to wash your feet. As you know, before the Last Supper, Jesus took the place of a servant to show he was no better then they were. As human beings, we are all equal. In marriage, you are equal partners. There are times when you may stand in awe of the other's greatness and rejoice in each other's triumphs. You may also be drawn closer together in times of sadness and defeat when you show unwavering support. This is not only life, it's the reason for marriage. As a married couple you give these experiences depth because you approach them with unconditional love. By washing your feet today, we are saying, I don't only stand before you, promising my love with a vow and a ring, but I'm kneeling before you, washing your feet, humbly accepting you as you are, not only with my words, but with my actions. My love is not just a promise, but an unconditional action of love. In humility, we as your husbands, commit ourselves to you today as equals. You bring all of who you are, and that is what makes us great together."

I added, "Let me read from the book of John 13:1–15." I stood to read the word.

It was just before the Passover Festival. Jesus knew that the hour had come for him to leave this world and go to the Father. Having loved his own who were in the world, he loved them to the end. The evening meal was in progress, and the devil had already prompted Judas, the son of Simon Iscariot, to betray Jesus. Jesus knew that the Father had put all things under his power, and that he had come from God and was returning to God; so he got up from the meal, took off his outer clothing, and wrapped a towel around his waist. After that, he poured water into a basin and began to wash his disciples' feet, drying them with the towel that was wrapped around him. He came to Simon Peter, who said to him, "Lord, are you going to wash my feet?" Jesus replied, "You do not realize now what I am doing, but later you will understand."

"No," said Peter, "you shall never wash my feet." Jesus answered, "Unless I wash you, you have no part with me." "Then, Lord," Simon Peter replied, "not just my feet but my hands and my head as well!" Jesus answered, "Those who have had a bath need only to wash their feet; their whole body is clean. And you are clean, though not every one of you." For he knew who was going to betray him, and that was why he said not everyone was clean. When he had finished washing their feet, he put on his clothes and returned to his place. "Do you understand what I have done for you?" he asked them. "You call me 'Teacher' and 'Lord,' and rightly so, for that is what I am. Now that I, your Lord and Teacher, have washed your feet, you also should wash one another's feet. I have set you an example that you should do as I have done for you.

Just like he said when he served the Last Supper, *Go and do likewise,* I resumed my position of kneeling before my wife. I don't know who started crying first—me or Camille—I just know talking was very difficult. I started by saying, "Baby, you've been my rock since Day One. You promised me that you'd always been in my corner." I dipped her right foot in the warm water. "And you've kept your word." I massaged her foot beneath the water. She's ticklish, so she kept flinching. I brought her left foot into the tub. "Today, I make the pledge before you and the Lord to be better than I have been. A better father. A better priest in our home. I'm going to serve you. I'll need you to pray for me. Thank you for your never-failing love." I was so focused on my pledge, I hadn't noticed the other men had already concluded theirs. They were just waiting on me. I wrapped Camille's feet in the towel.

We said our goodbyes and began the drive home. I knew Camille was in a good place. We were barely on the road for fifteen minutes before she was peacefully breathing, asleep. I could see the smile on her face from the corner of my eye.

Oh, I may just get some tonight.

I was right. She hadn't touched me like that in a long time.

17

The following week, I sat in Bible study listening to Sister Leah as she was teaching about the Prodigal Son. I knew her son had been battling a strong heroin addiction from his teens. Yet her love for him never waived. I listened intently as she taught from her heart.

"I'm not trying to make you feel bad or guilty for loving your prodigal so deeply. Romans 8:1 declares there is no condemnation, but I want to suggest to you the possibility of moving beyond your situation. I hope you understand that there is a better way; there is healing; there is restoration, but so much of this is up to you. I heard an evangelist once say, *No matter how many steps you have taken backwards or away from God, it only takes one step towards him.* The potter is ready to stick you back on the wheel; he can fix what is broken. Jesus is calling you to recommitment—surrender. You have tried it your way long enough; your kids, your spouse, your church, your community, they all need you to be whole and in right standing with the Lord. They need you to come back from the dead!"

She continued, "Jesus stood before his friend's tomb—weeping and angry. John 11:33 says, he *groaned* in the spirit and was *troubled*. The Greek word for *groaned* suggests Jesus' anger was related to the misery caused by sin, Satan, and death. Jesus informed the onlookers that they would see the glory of God. Jesus was there to perform a miracle; in this single act he would show his true power—the ability to give life when there is none. That death itself was no match for the Almighty Incarnate God! And he did it; with just a word."

I faded away for a moment. When I snapped back, I had written the following notes in my notebook:

Four things you need to realize about that moment;

1. Lazarus had been dead in the grave for four days;

2. He was bound from head to toe in the clothes of a dead man;

3. He could not see where he was going because he face was covered;

4. The tomb was just a hole in the wall—not a nice coffin or mausoleum—it was more likely just a hole that was large enough to slide the body in.

Sister Leah continued, "Bound, blind, and trapped in a hole, but this man responded to the Lord 's voice. Do you know why? Lazarus did not want to be dead anymore. On the first call, Lazarus got moving. He didn't say—*Hey, can somebody help me out of this hole?* No complaints that he could not see where he was going; he heard Jesus' voice and followed the simple instructions. No excuses. The directive was, *Come!* And Lazarus came. Jesus is still calling, *Come.* My question for you is—*What will you do?*"

"Will you continue to be bound by the grave clothes of sin, or will you respond to Jesus' call to new life? By word and deed, Jesus has shown us the path to live free from the power of sin. With Christ, you are more than a conqueror; you have been set free. Now live free!"

I thought of my own condition. *Hey, this is supposed to be a lesson on the Prodigal Son, right? I shouldn't be thinking about my sintimacy.*

"Only after Lazarus did his part did Jesus speak to those around to help him out of his bands, which shows the importance of accountability relationships. I can just imagine the joy in Lazarus' countenance when he saw the first faces of those who had taken the napkin from his face and who helped him get out of his mummy suit.

"I've told my son repeatedly that he has a choice. Either live for God and experience his presence, newness of life, and his protection; or live for yourself—and Satan—and take your chances against his wrath. It really seems like an easy decision. Make the choice to live your life God's way rather than your own."

I thought that to stay free from sintimacy we must actively wage war against the forces of darkness in our lives; we cannot afford to be passive. Yes, we have the victory through redemption, but we should be on the offensive of spiritual warfare. In his letter to Timothy, Paul put it this way:

Let everyone that nameth the name of Christ depart from iniquity. If you say you belong to God, then, you are no longer your own; if you call Jesus Lord, you must acknowledge His ownership.

Remember the story of the blind man of Bethsaida? Doesn't it seem peculiar that Jesus led the man out of the village? Most of his miracles were instantaneous, on-the-spot occurrences, but this required something different. You see, Bethsaida was under the curse of judgment for their lack of repentance—hint, hint. In Matthew's gospel, Jesus spoke quite sternly to the people of Bethsaida and the surrounding areas:

What horrors await you, Korazin and Bethsaida! For if the miracles I did in you had been done in wicked Tyre and Sidon, their people would have sat in deep repentance long ago, clothed in sackcloth and throwing ashes on their heads to show their remorse. I assure you, Tyre and Sidon will be better off on the judgment day than you! And you people of Capernaum, will you be exalted to heaven? No, you will be brought down to the place of the dead. For if the miracles I did for you had been done in Sodom, it would still be here today. I assure you, Sodom will be better off on the judgment day than you.

No wonder Jesus chose to remove this man from Bethsaida.

When Jesus removed His hands from the man's eyes, He asked him if he was able to see. The man admitted that he could see, but not clearly. Hmm—his eyes were still a bit dim. He acknowledged that everything was *not* alright. One of the biggest reasons why we do not get totally free is that we often do not admit that we are still wrestling with certain things. We want freedom from the big stuff but deny the existence of the little foxes or forget to acknowledge the multiple layers of sin. For instance, my addiction to pornography was not the only problem. There were multiple layers that needed repenting of: reading the magazines or visiting inappropriate sites on the internet—masturbation and adultery. To paraphrase Jesus, It's the thought that counts. Lying to my wife about what I was doing or where I had been—an out of control fantasy life that cheated my wife of my full sexual attention and focus. Need I go on?

This story of the Bethsaida blind man is the only biblical instance of Jesus performing a gradual miracle. After acknowledging that he still was not seeing clearly, Jesus again covered the man's eyes, but this time He turned the man's eyes toward heaven, and in that act of looking up, the man's sight was completely restored. The man's positioning and view of God had to change to aright his condition. He had to leave the place of cursing and then fix his gaze upon God, the one who could give him freedom.

Notice, now, Jesus' instructions to him after he was fully restored—the man was forbidden to ever return to Bethsaida nor was he even to share the news of his deliverance with anyone from the village. This means to completely sever the ties from your past life if you desire to stay free. Make the decision. As human beings, there is truly only one surety of living and that is the ever-present reality of death. Jesus can bring us to life, but we must live so that we do not enter death again.

I had realized that my relationship with Christ should change my behavior—I was made free to walk in the newness of life. When I counsel parents who are having difficulties with their teenagers or younger children, I often talk to them about teaching the children to see alternatives to their behaviors.

As parents, one of the first things we say to children is "No!" Think about it—when your child first started toddling around and went near the hot stove or touched the electrical outlet—you probably yelled "No!" and maybe scolded or even spanked the child to reinforce the command. What we often fail to do, however, is to give the child something that is OK to touch instead. Thankfully, the scriptures don't leave us hanging like that.

In the fourth chapter of his letter to the Ephesians, the Apostle Paul admonished the Christians who had learned the truth that is in Jesus to throw off the old, evil nature and former way of life, which is rotten through and through, full of lust and deception. He could have stopped there—those are really good instructions. Essentially he said, *Now that you know Christ, stop doing the things you used to do—that's not you anymore.* Second Timothy 2:21 admonishes us to view ourselves as vessels of honor for the Master's use. In this verse, Paul argues that living a pure and clean life is the appropriate way of life for believers—certainly an alternative lifestyle when you think of contemporary society.

In acknowledging Christ as Savior and Redeemer, I recognize his power to kill the effects of sin in my life. In fact, when I share in the power of his resurrection the old ways are made powerless. Through the power of His resurrection, our slavery to sin has been destroyed and we can faithfully weed out the fruit of sin in our lives, which includes a cancellation of the carnal, sinful human nature in which we are born. We do this by denying ourselves, applying self-control, refusing to allow our physical bodies used as instruments of unrighteousness, through spiritual warfare which includes fasting and consistent prayer. I had to remember that I was no longer in control, but was submitted to Christ.

I recall my first day of working at a particular job. My former boss sat me down and said, "In order to gain control, you need to give it up. Read Colossians 3—this chapter is paralleled with Ephesians 5. Both chapters deal with issues of submission. They talk about the roles of husbands, wives, and children. We often use these scriptures as doctrinal statements, but sometimes we miss the intent. Both chapters talk about submission—Ephesians 5 talks about living in and being submitted to the Spirit of God. In Colossians 3, the emphasis is on being filled with the Word of God. When the Word controls your life, you will be joyful, thankful, and submissive, and these are the same characteristics of the Spirit-filled Christian as explained in Ephesians 5. Submission to God is both symbolic of your yielding to Him as a sovereign deity, but practical in the sense that we are giving up control to an all-knowing, all-seeing, and ever-present God."

I was determined to be free from this thing. I made it up in my mind that my membership in the kingdom of God was conditionally based upon my faith, obedience, and love.

When I finally made it up in my own mind that I was *done* with living for my sintimacy of pornography, the Lord directed me to read, study, and ruminate on 1 Thessalonians 4:1-7:

Furthermore then we beseech you, brethren, and exhort you by the Lord Jesus, that as ye have received of us how ye ought to walk and to please God, so ye would abound more and more. For ye know what commandments we gave you by the Lord Jesus. For this is the will of God, even your sanctification, that ye should abstain from fornication: That every one of you should know how to possess his vessel in sanctification and honour; Not in the lust of concupiscence, even as the Gentiles which know not God: That no man go beyond and defraud his brother in any matter: because that the Lord is the avenger of all such, as we also have forewarned you and testified. For God hath not called us unto uncleanness, but unto holiness.

This scripture became my best friend—I recited it to myself daily, sometime four or more times a day. In the time of temptation, I focused on the part about possessing my vessel in sanctification and honor. I had to learn how to control and manage my own body in order to maintain my purity and consecration from the profane. It became life to me; the more I recited, the more I believed; the more I believed, the stronger I became; the stronger I became, the more I could stand firm in my liberty. There were certainly other scriptures that dealt with my particular problem, and I also studied them, but this one spoke to what I wanted to become—a vessel of honor.

Two weeks later, we got the surprise call that Sister Leah's son died of an accidental overdose. Rightfully, she was crushed. Pastor Craft and I officiated the funeral. He whispered something to her. I didn't mean to overhear or eavesdrop, but I'm glad I heard the message. As the funeral directors were closing the hearse, Pastor Craft leaned down to embrace Sister Leah and said, "God's grace is bigger than our addictions. If we don't believe that the size of God's grace is bigger than our problems, why would we serve Him?"

I sighed a breath of relief. After the repast, as we were sitting in his office, I told him, "Thank you for not throwing me away. I imagine other pastors would have stoned me."

He directed me to the Word.

"My actions were taken from Romans 5:20–21, "Where sin does abound, grace does much more abound…"

Camille has forgiven me. I can tell. Clean and righteous living has been a struggle. I would like to say it's been smooth sailing, but that would be a lie. The pull from the internet is real, but I believe the Lord has forgiven me and loves me still. I am now leading a Bible study at my church inviting men to live honestly—a sort of Truth. I'm not the same.

"What is this?" Camille questioned from behind my desk.

"What?" I sat in the easy chair with my back turned away from the chair.

"I'm serious. What is this? This site you've been looking at?"

I turned the chair around to face her at the desk. Camille seemed agitated. Her face was tight and her arms folded. She was staring at the screen. Her left hand on her heart. Her long sleeved black-and-white striped shirt bunched near her wrist. The wrinkles near her mouth demonstrated her anger.

What did she find? I haven't been doing anything bad.

Still my nerves kicked in causing a butterfly swarm in my belly.

"Look at this." Her arms defiantly folded and she sat back in the chair.

"What?" I whined.

Camille sat forward in the chair. Her mouth slightly agape, she pointed at the computer screen.

I had nervously stood up and approached the desk. I peered around the desk to try to see what I had done. "What?" Admittedly, the closer I neared the screen, the more I worried.

The golden brown, tanned skin of the bikini model stared back at me. Her red-thonged derriere busted from the picture. She had posed herself seductively with her right hand caught up in her long hair and her left coquettishly covering her breasts mimicking nudeness. I'm sure that she was nude or near nude if she turned around. I swallowed hard.

"I thought you weren't looking at this stuff anymore?" Camille's attitude boiled.

"I really haven't. What? It's nothing bad. All I see is a woman in a bikini. No big whoop."

"No big whoop? It might not be porn, but you can't honestly tell me you don't get turned on by this. Her booty is the biggest thing on the screen!"

She wasn't wrong. That girl was fine—quite nice looking! And I did enjoy looking at her. I mean her bottom was the perfect bubbled pear.

"And you probably don't think you've done anything wrong, I'll bet." Camille tersely argued with her arms folded.

Still, I defended against the gross mischaracterization. I had not done anything wrong.

"Did you contact Pastor Craft like he suggested?"

"For what? I did nothing wrong. I won't bother him. He's already too busy with church folks to have to worry about me." I stood above her as she remained seated.

"Bobby, it's exactly that attitude that causes problems. It's important that you think of this. It's the little foxes that spoil the vine, remember?"

"Camille, I hear you, but, truthfully, I have done nothing wrong. She's a woman in a bathing suit. She's not naked."

"I know she's not naked, but look at how provocatively she's dressed. It's not decent or holy. And you need to guard against this behavior. Remember, it's a battle of the mind."

Just then, she began rifling through the desk drawers. "Where is it," she wondered aloud. "I know it was in here. Oh, here it is." She pulled out the pamphlet we had been using at men's Bible study on the *Ten Disciplines*. She read from Discipline #3—The Mind:

"The potential of possessing the mind of Christ introduces the scandal of today's church—Christians who do not think Christianly, leaving our minds undisciplined."

I interrupted, "But babe…"

She countered, reading ever more loudly:

"The Apostle Paul understood this well: …whatever is true, whatever is honorable, whatever. Is just, whatever is pure, whatever is lovely,

whatever is commendable , if there is any excellence, if there is anything worthy of praise, think about these things. Each ingredient is a matter of personal choice."

"Seriously, babe. I don't need to be lectured right now."

Camille continued reading. *"You can never have a Christian mind without reading the Scriptures regularly because you cannot be influenced by that which you do not know."*

"It's like you don't even trust me."

"I'm trying to trust you. But think of my perspective. I open the computer and my eyes are assaulted by this girl's big butt practically leaping off the screen. How am I supposed to feel?" Her eyes glassed over as she teared up.

"Daddy, there's a monster under my bed. Can you come get him?" My young son came from his bedroom to the den. I welcomed the interruption.

"Yes, bud, I'll be right there. Just go back up, get in the bed, and I'll come chase him away."

"Can I have some warm milk? It'll help me sleep."

"Yep, you go upstairs, and I'll bring it to you." I turned away from Camille and sauntered into the kitchen, grabbed a pot, and pulled the milk from the refrigerator. As I placed the pot on the stove, I heard Camille call out from the den, "Uh, we're not done talking, sir."

"I've got to go take care of the baby. I'm on monster duty."

"Then we'll talk when you get back. Go take care of the monster."

I slowly trudged up the steps carrying the warm milk in a child safe sippy mug. I slipped into his room attempting a stealthy approach. I hoped he was asleep.

He wasn't sleeping at all. "Daddy, did you bring the milk?"

"I sure did, bud. Got it right here." I happily crouched in the bed behind him as he finished drinking. I did not make it very hot.

"Daddy, can you check under the bed for the monster?"

"Sure buddy." I got down on my knees beside the bed and briefly peeked underneath. I saw nothing but dirty underwear and balled-up socks. I made a mental note to have him clean under his bed tomorrow.

"There's no monster under here. Just close your eyes and go to sleep."

"Daddy, I have to go to the potty."

I knew what he was trying to do. "Boy, go to the bathroom and then get in this bed and go to sleep. I'm not playing." I tried to sound stern.

He ran off to go potty.

I waited for him to return. "OK, son. Now I have to go downstairs. You go to bed."

"Yes, Daddy."

I turned on his night light and withdrew from his room. When I got back downstairs, I had hoped just to relax. "Whew, that boy is too much."

Camille continued like I had never left.

"Don't let your good be evil spoken of," Camille advised, ignoring my comment.

Ugh. I thought this was over.

"Of a truth, dear. You really need to be careful. Sincerely, guard your heart. Remember what the scriptures say, *with all diligence, for out of it flow are the issues of life.* Perhaps the Proverbs of the wisest man in history should sway you."

I fail to see Solomon as the wisest example of Christendom. Didn't he have 300 concubines and 700 wives? Solomon's marital decisions were in direct violation of God's law, and there were consequences.

"Bobby, do you hear me talking to you?" Camille's angry words chilled the air.

"Huh? What? Yes, I heard you," I answered.

"Then tell me what I said." Camille knows I don't listen well.

"You said I should follow Solomon's advice," I said, then rashly added, "I always thought wisdom was applied knowledge; it helps us make decisions that honor the Lord and agree with the Scriptures. Solomon's book of *Proverbs* is filled with practical counsel on how to follow the Lord. But Solomon also wrote the *Song of Solomon,* which presents a beautiful picture of what God intends marriage to be. So, King Solomon *knew* what was right, even if he didn't always follow the right path.

"Speaking of the *Song of Solomon,* I believe that's part of my problem. The husband in that story totally loved his bride. He said

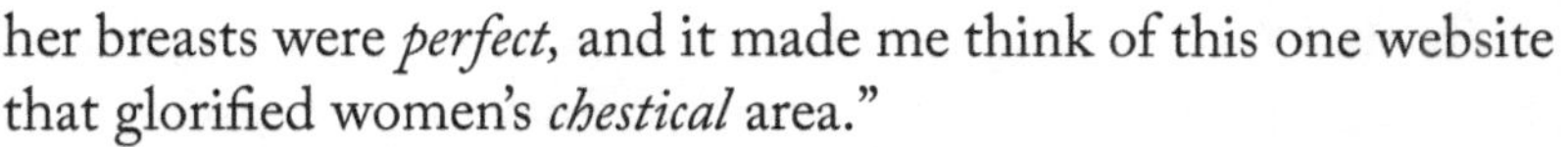

her breasts were *perfect,* and it made me think of this one website that glorified women's *chestical* area."

Seriously though, porn is some new phenomenon that started with me. No sir, this war has been raging for thousands of years. In A.D. 79 Pompeii, a first-century Roman city was destroyed by a volcanic eruption. When the ruins were unearthed, they revealed a two-story brothel. Found in each room were erotic wall paintings depicting various sexual acts. *This beast has been raging for millennia. I feel powerless to overcome it.*

As if she was reading my mind, Camille asserted "Stop feeding it with nonsense like this. It's like Sister Ruby said, 'Don't wash your garments in polluted water.'"

I'll admit. That one made me think. "I hear you, baby, and I will do better." I yawned and stretched and scratched my head, "Now can we please just go to bed."

†††

The kids had filed into our fellowship hall for youth group. It was just another day. Teenage hormones floated throughout the church as the middle and high school ruffians gathered. Almost immediately, the questions started.

"What are we doing today?" Russ inquired.

"Yeah, what's the plan?" Jack added.

I was not in the habit of giving details or plans beforehand, mostly out of fear that they'd begin complaining before we'd even gotten a chance to start.

"You'll see in a minute," I said with a smile.

It was a hot August day, and the kids already seemed testy. I stood at the front of the room. "How about we make sundaes?"

"Ooh, yes!" Teen eyes widened all over the room as my team members brought in supplies from the kitchen area. They smiled as they imagined getting the sweet treats. One boy licked his lips.

I invited the kids up. As they gathered around the tables with ice cream scoops and plastic bowls, the other adult volunteers began spreading plastic tarps onto the center of the floor. The kids moaned, especially when they saw the bags being taped down.

"Uh oh. What's going on?" Tanya knew something was amiss. She had been a youth group participant for a couple years.

I stood at the front and invited everyone to get into teams of two. "Don't worry, guys. It'll be fun, I promise. Now, the task at hand it to finish your bowl of ice cream by lying on the ground head-to-head and spoon-feeding the sundae over your head into the mouth of your partner. This is a race to feed each other like this and eat their ice cream before any other twosome. First two to finish wins a prize.

"But, I don't know what she made or what she put into her sundae." Rhonda questioned her choice of partner mostly. I had not discussed what the challenge was before they made their sundaes. The students all started with plain, vanilla ice cream. Then some chose to add nuts, cookie crumbles, gummy candies, chocolate syrup or caramel. The kids had made quite a mess with the whipped cream canisters.

"Alright, lie on your backs head-to-head. The whole point of this little exercise is working together to accomplish a goal. Trade bowls with your partner. That way, you get to eat the sundae you chose to make. Is that better, Rhonda?"

"Yeah, that's good."

"Okay. On your mark, get set, and go!"

Arms scooped and extended backwards. The first spoonful I don't think actually reached anybody's mouth. I laughed as vanilla ice cream fell on eyebrows and foreheads. There were screams and grunts.

"That's nasty!" J.D. screamed aloud. "I got brain freeze!"

The boy nicknamed B-rad G—he looked just like the would-be rapper from *Malibu's Most Wanted*—and his partner Jaquon were rocking right from the start. After a few slip ups, they seemed to fall into a rhythm. They both served the last scoop to each other to win the contest.

"We have our winners. B-rad and Jaquon!"

B-rad asked innocently, "What did we win? What's our prize?"

"Bragging rights. That's it." I slapped each of them a disgruntled high five.

"Go get cleaned up in the bathroom and come back and take your seat out here on the plastic."

"That was fun," Taiko admitted. "Me and James almost beat y'all." She jokingly pushed back at Jaquon.

Jaquon shot back at her. "Yeah, but you didn't."

"I'm gonna have to wash my hair tonight. We got ice cream all in it," Jamey complained as he came out of the bathroom.

"Yup. I'm all sticky," Alisha whined.

While they were cleaning up in the bathroom, the other adults and I transitioned the play area to a learning area. I again stood at front.

"Alright, play time is over. Now it's time to get serious. You know, I was young once. I remember being a teenager and comparing myself to my brothers. They were the cool ones. They got all the girls. Me, I was the church boy. But I never really learned to appreciate my identity as a saved kid." I paused to give them some time to imagine. "I had a lot of bad self-talk. I never felt good enough, smart enough, or pretty enough. How many of you have ever told yourself something that you did wrong or that some part of you was wrong?" Kids raised their hands across the room in silence.

"Most of you have heard of the Creation story featuring Adam and Eve, yeah? Do you remember after God created or developed man? What did He say about man?"

"He said he was good," Annie offered from the rear of the room.

"He sure did. He said the same thing about Eve after he created her. It's probably been a long time since you've referred to yourself that way, huh? The Apostle Paul talked about Jesus I think with us in mind. He said in 1 Corinthians 5:21 *For he hath made him to be sin for us, who knew no sin; that we might be made the righteousness of God in him.* Imagine that for a second. Repeat those words, 'I am the righteousness of God.' Even with your mistakes and on-purposes, you are the righteousness of God in Christ Jesus.

"How many of you have ever heard of positive self-talk? I was listening to a song recently, and it really spoke to me. The song is titled "Greatly Blessed, Highly Favored." I'm going to teach it to you now. I want this song to be an affirmation of the way to talk to yourself. Say it to yourself in the mirror if you have to. OK, repeat after me. Greatly blessed…"

We did a call and response of the chorus. As the kids repeated, I moved to the computer and played the video featuring the Gaither Vocal Band. The country twang began, and the middle-aged men began singing those words I had taught the kids. Soon, the group was joined by members of the Gatlin Brothers. I instructed, "Ignore the country music style and focus on the words to tell yourselves." I let the music continue to its conclusion. The kids had repeated it over a few times.

"B-rad. What does the song say, in your own words?"

"It says, even though I'm not perfect, I'm still a blessed child of God."

"Yup! Remember that, and when the devil tries to make you feel bad for something you've done or something you are, tell him back to his face that you are greatly blessed and highly favored. Tell him yes, you are imperfect, but you are forgiven. Tell him you are a child of God. When someone tries to remind you of ways you may have failed, repeat these words to them. You are the *righteousness of God*. Let that sink in. God is not mad at you. You can answer back, and what should you say, Jaquon?"

"I'm highly favored and greatly blessed. I'm a forgiven child of God."

"Remember who you are. It's okay to tell your detractors, *Please be patient with me. God ain't through with me yet.* Let's stand up and let one of our adult volunteers pray as we are dismissed. Brother J, how about you close us out in prayer?"

"Heavenly Father, thank you for this simple word tonight. Pastor Bobby J reminded us of your great love for all of us. Remind us daily of your immense love for each of us. Teach us to love ourselves as you have loved us. Teach us to be kind to ourselves and each other. Please forgive us when we doubt you and forgive us when we speak down to ourselves. Tonight, I am proud to say I am yours. I am happy to leave this place with this thought—greatly blessed, highly favored, imperfect but forgiven. I'm a child of God. Amen."

About the Author

Brian C. Johnson honors the struggles and accomplishments of the ordinary citizens who launched the Civil Rights Movement by committing himself personally and professionally to the advancement of multicultural and inclusive education.

He earned both bachelor's and master's degrees in English from California University of Pennsylvania, and a Ph.D. in communications media and instructional technology at Indiana University of Pennsylvania in December 2016. Brian is the co-author of *Reel Diversity: A Teacher's Sourcebook* (2008), winner of the 2009 Phillip Chinn Book Award by the National Association for Multicultural Education and a revised edition in 2015, and *We've Scene It All Before: Using Film Clips in Diversity Awareness Training* (2009). His youth Bible study, *Finding God in the Bathroom,* was published in 2020.

Brian serves on the ministry team at Revival Tabernacle in Watsontown, Pennsylvania where he is the youth pastor. He is a gifted teacher and enjoys sharing hope and joy with those to whom he ministers.